SEA SALT CARAMEL MURDER

A MAPLE HILLS COZY MYSTERY #4

WENDY MEADOWS

1

Holding an umbrella over her head, Nikki studied the *Open Sea Queen*. The sight of the cruise ship made her stomach cringe. Expecting to see a beautiful, modern ship with every luxury imaginable, she was instead staring at a boat that resembled a run-down merchant ship on its last leg. "Uh, Hawk, are you sure this is our ship?" she asked.

Hawk drew in a deep breath. Taking his eyes away from the ship, he focused on the stormy harbor. The water was rough, choppy, and angry, as if hungry for ships to devour. Overhead, the sky was low, dark, and filled with heavy rain. Of course, he was in Seattle, and it rained in Seattle all the time. But still, Hawk thought, daring to glance at Nikki, he had expected sunny skies and a cruise ship filled with all the trimmings. "Thing looks like it's about to sink," he admitted.

"Nonsense," Herbert told Hawk and slapped him on the back, "this ship has character. Unlike the ships we see today that are all similar in style, the ship you see before you is one of a kind...delightful in every sense."

Nikki looked over her shoulder at Lidia. Lidia simply shrugged her shoulders. "Well," Nikki said, feeling rain striking her light yellow dress as the wind began to pick up, "perhaps we should get aboard?"

Hawk hesitated. Sure, he wanted to go on a cruise, and the thought of seeing Alaska sounded great, but something was wrong. The idea of being out on the open sea with Nikki, though, caused him to ignore his gut. Things were going great between him and Nikki. The last thing he wanted was for an old rundown ship to stand in his way. Shifting the umbrella from his right hand to his left, he quickly wiped rain off his blue and white long-sleeved jersey and bit down on his lower lip. "Yeah, I guess we should."

"Too bad Tori couldn't come," Lidia said, standing under the umbrella Herbert was holding over her head. Looking to her left and then to her right, she examined the wooden dock the ship was resting against. Beneath her feet, she could feel the rough waters growling at her. Turning around, she looked at a rusty two-story metal building that served as the shipping company's center of operations. "Herbert, maybe we should—"

Herbert nudged Lidia in the side with his elbow. "No," he said in a stern voice. Dressed in a dark blue suit with a pipe in his mouth, he felt like a man preparing to take on the untamed sea, a daring sea captain raring for an adventure. "What we have here is a 1957 Chevy, a classic.

But the world wants one of those new plastic cars that looks pretty, but in reality, is simply junk."

Lidia sighed. "Well, I am wearing my new dress," she caved in.

Nikki grinned and then winked at Lidia. Lidia looked dazzling in the soft pink she was wearing. Sure, later on, they would all put on warmer clothes, but for now, the rainy weather was just warm enough to hint at needing nothing more than a simple long-sleeved shirt or dress.

Herbert began to speak again but was quickly interrupted when a Chinese man in his early thirties brushed by, carrying a green duffel bag. "Out of my way," he said in a tough voice.

"Jerk!" Lidia yelled.

The Chinese man ignored Lidia. Oblivious to the rain and the fact that his black suit was soaking wet, he aimed toward the gangplank, yanked a ticket out of his front pocket, showed it to a young man holding an umbrella, and hurried aboard.

Hawk hesitated to go after the man. What would he do? Slug the guy? No, he thought, watching a slow drip of passengers move aboard the ship like lost stories, each wandering around without an ending. "Let's go," he said, forcing a weak smile to his face.

"That's what I like to hear," Herbert said and clapped Hawk on the back again. Bending down, he grabbed a brown suitcase. Lidia gave Nikki a worried look, picked up a white suitcase, and followed Herbert to the gangplank.

Picking up her own suitcase, Nikki focused her attention

on Hawk. "Don't feel bad, okay? How could we have known?"

"Next time I see my friend who gave me these lousy tickets, I'm going to slug him," Hawk grumbled. "Nikki, I should have checked the tickets out. I'm sorry."

"Don't be," Nikki said, offering Hawk a gentle smile. Looking at the ship, she shrugged her shoulders. "It's never good to judge a book by its cover. Who knows, maybe Herbert is right? Maybe the ship is a diamond in the rough. Come on, let's get on board before we drown out here."

"Yeah," Hawk said, grabbing his green duffel bag. "Lead the way, Captain Bates."

Walking over to the gangplank, Nikki paused. With nervous eyes, she looked down at the dark gray, deep water. A simple wooden platform that creaked with every step was all that stood between her and a watery death. Not even a seasoned swimmer would stand a chance against the angry waters slapping at the ship. Cautiously, she eased her way onto the platform and, step by step—wishing she had on tennis shoes instead of high heels—she moved forward.

"Ticket, please," said a young man standing just inside the ship's entry. The young man, to Nikki's surprise, was wearing a very nice white and blue sailor's suit with a bright golden name tag. He had a very neat haircut, a polite and helpful demeanor, and a smile that helped relax her. Surely, she thought, handing over her ticket, if anything was wrong with the ship, the nice young man welcoming passengers wouldn't appear so relaxed. "Cabin 7A, second deck." The young man smiled at Nikki, handing her a room key.

Looking over her shoulder, she smiled at Hawk, tucked away her umbrella, and boarded the ship. Stepping into a brightly lit passageway, she drew in a deep breath of air that smelled like pumpkin spice. Waiting for Hawk, she took a few seconds to admire the white marble lining the passage and the dark burgundy walls. At the end of it, she saw a wooden door standing open. "Herbert, you may be right," she smiled, feeling as if she had stepped onto the Titanic, without the sinking, of course.

"All set," Hawk said, stepping up behind Nikki. Admiring the passageway, he felt the anxiety eating away at him diminish. "Don't judge a book by its cover," he winked at Nikki.

"Come on, you guys," Lidia called, "let's get to our cabins. I'm starving and I want to find the dining hall."

"Shall we?" Nikki asked Hawk.

"We shall, ma'am," Hawk answered.

Walking down the passageways, Nikki stepped through the wooden door into a gorgeous passenger lounge. "Oh Hawk, it's beautiful," she said, looking down at a burgundy carpet. Drawing in a scent of cigar smoke mixed with pumpkin spice, she closed her eyes. For a few seconds, she imagined being a passenger on the Titanic.

"It's nice, that's for sure," Hawk agreed. Examining the lounge, he let his eyes float around. The space was designed with an early twentieth-century look. Old-fashioned lamps hung from light green walls (holding electric lights of course, but still authentic in appearance). Brilliantly carved wooden beams stood spaced apart from one another, offering comfortable passage while promising strength and security. Even the elevator was old-fashioned. Hawk watched a young man open a cage-style door, allowing the rude Chinese man to step on.

"What did I tell you?" Herbert said in a delighted voice, shaking rain from his umbrella. "Now, let us forget the world exists for a few days and soak in this wonderful atmosphere."

Unable to hide her joy, Lidia nuzzled up next to her husband and agreed. "I'm aboard, Captain," she promised and kissed Herbert on his cheek.

"Well...yes," Herbert blushed. "We'll meet back here in, say, one hour, and go have dinner," he told Nikki and Hawk.

"Sounds good," Hawk agreed, casually studying each passenger and employee in the lounge. It wasn't crowded, but there were enough people to realize that a healthy-sized crew was needed. Glancing at Nikki, Hawk saw her open her eyes and nod at Herbert.

"One hour," Lidia promised and hurried to the elevator with Herbert.

"I'm so grateful to see Lidia happy," Nikki told Hawk. "Lidia has been a true friend, one of the best."

"She's a rare one," Hawk agreed.

Spotting a tall man with a thick white beard walking around the lobby and greeting passengers, Nikki nodded at him. "That must be the captain."

Hawk followed Nikki's eyes. He spotted a man, who he guessed was in his early sixties, wearing a dark white and blue uniform that radiated authority and intelligence. The man, Hawk saw, had the face of someone who knew the ways of the world quite well. "Hello, I'm Captain Ebenezer Mayfield. And no, before you ask, I am not a scrooge," the man said, introducing himself to Nikki and Hawk.

Nikki smiled and shook Captain Mayfield's hand. The scent of cigar smoke emanated from his thick white beard like old sailors rowing back from the shore, hungry for their ship. "I'm Nikki Bates."

"Hawk Daily," Hawk said, shaking Captain Mayfield's hand. "Detective Hawk Daily."

"Yes," Captain Mayfield said and shook Hawk's hand. "I was told a man of the law would be a guest on this voyage. I am delighted. It's not often that I can go cheap on security and save a few dollars," he finished and then tipped a wink at Nikki.

Nikki laughed at the joke. Hawk, always one to have a good sense of humor instead of having thin skin, laughed too. "Well, don't be mad if I give you a bill before I leave," he joked back.

"Alas," Captain Mayfield said, stepping into a poor seaman's voice, "we men of the sea are paid only with long letters to home from seasick hearts."

"In that case, I'll work for free," Hawk replied. Picking up his duffel bag he motioned to the elevator. "Well, we need to get settled in."

Captain Mayfield looked at Nikki. "May I request that you sit at my table tonight when dinner is served?" he asked her in a warm, soothing voice.

"Sure," Nikki smiled, "but only if you let me bring this big lug with me."

"At no extra charge," Captain Mayfield promised.

"Good grief," Hawk moaned as they wandered away to the elevator. "Not even on the ship ten minutes and I'm already playing second fiddle to grandpa."

Nikki giggled and caught up with Hawk. After riding the elevator down to her deck, she walked down a passageway and found her cabin, which was located at the far end on the right. Putting down her suitcase, she studied the wooden door before her. The door, like the one in the passenger lounge, was heavy and made of quality wood. "I feel like I've walked back in time."

Using the key in her right hand, Nikki opened the door. Picking up the suitcase, she stepped into a stateroom that resembled a palace. The floors were dark wood; the walls, like those of the passageway, were burgundy; the ceiling held old wooden beams with sprinkles of brilliance. In the middle of the room stood a large bed with silk bed curtains wrapped around it. On the back wall, she saw a wooden door leading into a bathroom. What Nikki didn't see was a television. The only modern touch was a white phone sitting on a chest of drawers carved to resemble a treasure chest. "My goodness," Nikki said, taken aback by the beauty of the room. Closing the door, she walked to her bed and placed her suitcase down onto a thick green quilt. "This ship is amazing."

Walking to the bathroom door, she opened it, found an old-fashioned light switch, and activated it. Dim, romantic light filled a room with hardwood floors holding a bronze claw-foot bathtub with white roses painted on the side, a white porcelain toilet, and a bronze sink attached to a wooden barrel. Impressed, Nikki walked back into the room and examined the furnishings. "Chair, couch, a grand bed…" she whispered. "Yes, I could live in this room the rest of my life."

2

After changing into a green and white long-sleeved dress, Nikki grabbed her purse and exited her cabin. Returning to the lounge, she wandered over to a small store area. A pretty young girl with short red hair was standing behind a wooden counter. "Can I help you with anything?" she asked in a polite voice.

"A bottle of water?" Nikki asked, spotting a cooler holding refreshing drinks.

"Of course," the girl said and quickly retrieved Nikki a bottle of water.

"How much?"

"All expenses are included in your ticket," the girl smiled at Nikki.

"I see," Nikki smiled back gratefully, taking the bottle of water and opening it. "I have to say, from the outside of the ship you would have never guessed the inside was so lovely."

"Oh yes," the girl quickly agreed, "the owner of *Open*

Sea Queen is very old-fashioned. Rumor is his grandfather was one of the men who helped design the Titanic...that's a rumor, of course."

"Why a rumor?"

The young girl shrugged her shoulders. "The owner of this ship is a very private man. No one really knows that much about him and..." The young girl stopped talking. "Oh my, I've been babbling. I'm not supposed to...uh, I didn't mean—"

"I understand," Nikki assured the girl and patted her hand.

"Thanks," the girl told Nikki. "This is only my second voyage. I'm still getting used to this ship and being a part of the crew."

"Well," Nikki said, sipping her water, "you couldn't ask for a better job. A lovely ship that sails the shores of Alaska. My, what I wouldn't have given as a young lady to be in your shoes."

"Hey there," Hawk said, walking up to Nikki, "all settled?"

"In my palace," Nikki smiled.

"You too, huh? My stateroom looks like a prince should live in it instead of a detective who never gets caught up on the hockey scores."

"Princes come in all shapes and sizes," Nikki told Hawk, spotting Lidia and Herbert. "When is lunch served?" she asked the girl.

"We'll be departing in less than twenty minutes," the girl explained. "Lunch will be served one hour after departure."

Hawk checked his watch. "It's 11:10 am," he told Nikki. "We have some time."

"We better get Lidia a candy bar, then," Nikki said. Feeling relaxed, she pushed every worry from her mind. Glancing at Hawk, she felt safe. "I'm glad we came. I needed to get away."

"So did I," Hawk agreed. "I have to admit, Nikki, at times I'm feeling my age. When I tangled with Judge Stewart's son, it took every ounce of energy I had to take that guy down. I left New York because I was beginning to feel old before my time. All I want is a nice, quiet cruise."

"And a nice, quiet little town to go home to," Nikki added.

"Hey, you two," Lidia said, walking up with Herbert. Smiling, Lidia quickly told Nikki all about her cabin. "Fit for a king. Oh, how I wish Tori could be here! But no, she insisted on staying and tending to the store."

"I wish she were here, too," Nikki told Lidia. "We're about to set sail in twenty minutes. Lunch will be served at 12:30. You might want to grab a snack."

Lidia patted the gray and blue pocketbook she was carrying. "I read the dining schedule in my cabin. I came prepared. I am loaded down with peanut butter crackers and—"

Lidia stopped talking. "What's wrong?" Nikki asked.

"It's him," she whispered. With her eyes, she pointed to

the rude Chinese man who had brushed past Herbert on the dock.

Nikki found the Chinese man stepping off the guest elevator. He looked around and then hung a right, walking toward the ship's dining area. "Look," Hawk said, "let's not paint a bulls-eye on some guy who lacks manners. Herbert, I asked about the gym. I was thinking we could go work up a sweat before lunch."

"Oh," the girl told Nikki, "I forgot. Tea and muffins are being served in the tea room, if anyone is interested."

"I am anxious to break in the steam room. I don't want tea and muffins," Herbert told Hawk. "Ladies, the gym comes equipped with a pool, a steam room, an exercise room, and a small lounge. Would you like to join us?"

"Not me," Lidia said, putting the pack of peanut butter crackers back into her purse. "I get all the exercise I want at home. I think I'll go have some tea and muffins. Nikki, are you with me?"

"Sure," Nikki said, looking in the direction the Chinese man disappeared.

Hawk caught Nikki's mind beginning to wander off into an area that concerned him. "Please, Nikki, let's have a nice, quiet, peaceful cruise. Whatever you're thinking, stop. We're on this ship to relax, remember?"

"Huh? Oh, yeah, sure," Nikki replied, returning her attention back to him. Offering an innocent smile, she shooed Hawk away. "Go work out, okay?"

"Lidia, watch her," Hawk pleaded.

"We'll meet you ladies in one hour," Herbert said and walked away with Hawk.

As soon as Hawk and Herbert were out of sight, Nikki bit down on her lower lip. "No," Lidia said, seeing the look in Nikki's eye. "Nice and quiet, okay?"

"Okay," Nikki promised. "I'm just a little curious as to who that Chinese man is."

"I don't know his name," the girl told Nikki, taking a risk, "but I do know he was on the last cruise."

"Are you sure?" Nikki asked, spinning around.

"Oh dear," Lidia sighed. Before the girl could answer, Lidia grabbed Nikki's arm and pulled her away. "Nice and quiet. We'll forget all about Mr. Rude and enjoy ourselves, dear."

Nikki allowed Lidia to drag her into a lovely passageway with signs giving directions to the ship's dining rooms, entertainment room, library, sitting room, smoking room, and tea room. "Let's go to the tea room," Lidia told Nikki. "We can relax, sip tea, eat muffins, chat about girly stuff, and rest."

Catching her detective instincts trying to dominate her need to relax, Nikki looked at Lidia. "Oh dear, Lidia, I'm sorry. Old habits are hard to break. Tea and muffins sound great."

3

Lidia began to speak but stopped when the Chinese man stepped out of a public restroom into the passageway. Without saying a word, he looked at Lidia and Nikki and then hurried away. "Say, he wasn't carrying a briefcase when we last saw him," Lidia quickly pointed out, and then, like a guilty cat caught with its paws in the milk bowl, she looked at Nikki. "You're rubbing off on me."

Before Nikki could speak, a second man stepped out of the bathroom. The man was Captain Mayfield. "Ladies, I better get us under way." He smiled and vanished down the hallway on fast legs.

"Lidia, take me to the tea room before I follow the captain," Nikki begged.

Lidia quickly grabbed Nikki's hand and pulled her into an elegant tea room lined with antique furnishings and open bay windows looking out into the stormy harbor. Two women in their early sixties, both wearing vintage

European maid uniforms, greeted Lidia and Nikki. One of the women escorted them to a table next to a marble fireplace. "Today's teas are peppermint, lemon, English breakfast..." The woman politely began to name off the teas being served and finished with the muffins.

Nikki glanced around the tea room. She and Lidia were the only occupants. "Uh, peppermint tea with a blueberry muffin," she told the woman.

"Lemon tea with a bran muffin," Lidia put in her order. Reading the woman's name tag, she added: "June, can you also bring me some honey if you have any?"

"Of course," June told Lidia, "I drink my tea that way myself."

As soon as June was out of earshot, Nikki spoke. "I'm going to forget what I saw. I'm here to relax, relax with my friends."

"You say that in a very pained voice," Lidia told Nikki. Looking out at the stormy harbor, she wrinkled her nose. "Honey, let's just enjoy our time on this lovely ship. What are the chances a crime—or murder—will take place? That rude Chinese man may just be ship security or something."

Nikki considered Lidia's suggestion. "It's possible," she agreed. Taking a very deep breath, she put her purse down on the table and smiled. "Silly me, here I am ready to dive into an empty pool."

"You and me both," Lidia laughed. "Now, let's talk about girl stuff. You must tell me where you purchase your dresses and where you get your shoes."

Nikki smiled. "I order from a store online," she admitted and dove into a full conversation about dresses and shoes as the ship slowly began to get underway and move out into a stormy sea. She sipped her tea and munched on her muffin and allowed her mind to forget about what she saw in the hallway.

As Nikki and Lidia talked, the Chinese man walked back to his cabin. Once securely inside, he locked himself in the cabin's bathroom, placed the suitcase down on the counter, and opened it. A sea of diamonds appeared before his eyes. With an angry hand, he snatched up a single diamond, examined it, and then growled. Throwing the diamond down, he slammed the briefcase shut. "Play games with me..." he whispered through clenched teeth.

see the Chinese man enter the dining room, spot the captain, and then leave. But Lidia did. She didn't say a word. "Hawk, what did you do with your Ford?"

"Well," Hawk laughed to himself as his mind wandered back in time, "I sold that old Ford to a junk dealer and bought a used motorcycle. I was getting ready to leave for college, and I wanted to look cool. I couldn't be seen driving a rusted Ford around, no matter how the inside looked."

"What's so funny about that?" Nikki asked.

"Well," Hawk explained, "my first day on campus I crashed the motorcycle into a tree. I was kinda looking at this girl, you see..."

Herbert and Lidia laughed. "We understand."

Nikki shook her head at Hawk. "Boys will be boys," she sighed.

"Boys will be boys with a broken shoulder," Hawk added. Nikki laughed. It was good to see Nikki laugh. Hawk stared into her beautiful face with eyes that swore he was seeing a part of Heaven.

Nikki began to tease Hawk but was interrupted when she saw a man wearing a black and white uniform rush into the dining room, hightail it to the captain's table, and hand him a piece of paper. Nikki watched Captain Mayfield take the paper and read it. Captain Mayfield's face went from pleasant to alarmed in a matter of seconds. Excusing himself from the guests sitting at his table, he calmly left the dining room, even though his body language was stiff and tense. "Now, what was that all about?"

Hawk put down the fork in his hand. He had watched Captain Mayfield's face grow concerned when the second officer in command handed him a weather report. "I'll go find out," Hawk said, standing up. Nikki began to stand up, but Hawk shook his head. "No," he said in a firm voice. "Nikki, if it's something serious, I'll come and get you."

"Let him go," Lidia urged Nikki.

"Hurry," Nikki pleaded.

Hawk, not wanting to draw attention to himself, excused himself from the table. He casually exited the dining room. Looking to his left and then to his right, he searched for Captain Mayfield. Hearing voices coming from his right, he eased down a passageway that spoke of time and better days, days when people were more real in heart rather than mind. "Sir, this storm system is moving in from behind us. We can't return to port," Hawk heard a man tell Captain Mayfield in a worried voice.

"Contact the local ports and see if we can swing in for a stop," Captain Mayfield replied, staring at the weather report in his hand. Shaking his head, he moved to a porthole and studied the darkening night outside. The seas were rough but manageable. The waves were angry, bitter, and deadly; dark and filled with a hunger rising up from a deep abyss.

"I already did," Captain Mayfield's second-in-command replied. The man's name was Brody Lane. Short, plump, and well into his late forties, Brody Lane resembled a clown rather than a man who had spent his life daring the open seas. Yet, Hawk saw, peering around the corner of the passageway in order to see better, the man also held a very fine, intelligent expression underlined with a cleverness he couldn't quite put his finger on. "All ports are full. This storm is pushing the ships in."

"No one has room for us?" Captain Mayfield asked in an unbelieving tone. "Come now, this is impossible. You get on the line and force someone to put out a welcome mat for us."

"Well, we could try to return to home port," Brody suggested.

"Out of the question. If we do, every passenger will request refunds. Absolutely not. We will find a port to dock in long enough for the storm to pass and—"

"Captain Mayfield, if I may sir...perhaps we should try and stay ahead of the storm system? We can push farther out to sea and then swing back in," Brody politely interrupted. "The storm system is driving northwest. We may lose a few hours, but—"

Captain Mayfield squeezed his hands into two tight fists and struck the wall. "You dare question me, Lane?" he exploded. Hawk watched Captain Mayfield turn around. The man's face was no longer pleasant. Now Captain Mayfield's face was consumed with a deadly anger that caused Hawk to place his hand on his service gun strapped around his ankle. "You will stay on course. If no one will take us in, we will ride the storm, is that clear?"

"Ride the storm?" Brody asked, backing away from Captain Mayfield. "That's insane. The swells are forecasted to—"

"Need I remind you who is captain?" Captain Mayfield

hollered at Brody. "Listen to me, you pathetic drunk. No one dared—*dared*—take you on as their second-in-command. The tragedy of the *Blue Pearl* has destroyed your life, Lane. But I took you in, didn't I? I made you second-in-command, didn't I? And if you want to remain second-in-command, you better obey my every order, are we clear? If you refuse, you can tell your wife that it was your fault that you can no longer pay for her medical treatments."

Like a beaten dog, Brody looked down at his feet. "Yes, Captain. I'm very sorry, sir. I didn't mean to question you. I...you have been very kind to me and my wife. I will keep us on course, sir."

Captain Mayfield stared at Brody, took a few breaths, and then put on a fake smile. Patting Brody on the shoulder, he nodded his head. "That's a good man, Lane. I know that I can trust you. I see good things for you in the future. You have always served me well. I will see to it that you get your bonus. Now, get back to the bridge. I will join you shortly. And not a word to anyone. If the passengers begin to ask questions, we will assure them that we have sailed into a minor storm which is of no grave concern, are we clear?"

"Yes, sir," Brody said and hurried away with his tail between his legs.

5

Hawk shook his head, walked back to the dining room, and sat down. The smell of delicious food, the sight of people laughing, talking, and enjoying themselves, the sounds of dinnerware clanging and clattering—it all faded away. Like a man in a tunnel, he saw only Captain Mayfield's angry, deceitful face in his mind. "What is it?" Nikki asked Hawk, worried. Reading Hawk's face, she could clearly see that he had come upon some very disturbing information.

Herbert put down his fork. Lidia leaned forward on her elbows. "Speak to us," she told Hawk.

"What did you find out?" Herbert insisted. The expression on Hawk's face troubled him. Never the type of man to allow panic to overwhelm his composure, he stared at Hawk with forced patience.

"Storm is coming in from behind us," Hawk whispered. Glancing around to ensure other passengers were not focused on his table, he continued. "Mayfield has ordered his second-in-command to keep the ship on course. Seems this storm system is pushing all the ships in, and all the ports are filling up."

"What does that mean?" Lidia asked, confused.

Hawk looked at Nikki and then to Lidia. "Mayfield's second-in-command wanted to take this ship farther out to sea, farther west, to move away from the storm. The storm is moving north, right on our tail, it seems. Mayfield wouldn't hear of it. Mayfield has given the order to ride the storm if we get caught in it."

Nikki studied Hawk's face. "Hawk, there's something else, isn't there?"

Hawk nodded. "Something about swells...Mayfield's second-in-command...I remember seeing this man earlier. His last name is Lane; he mentioned something about swells and seemed awful worried about the forecasts. I'm guessing we're not talking kiddie-pool swells, guys. Mayfield cut Lane off before he could finish, though."

"Oh dear," Lidia gasped. "Hawk, you're a cop. Go tell that man to return us to Seattle this instant."

"That's what Lane suggested, but Mayfield refused. If he returns this ship to home port, he's worried all the passengers will request refunds. But my gut tells me that's a lie. The man has an agenda."

Nikki pushed her mind back in time a few hours. She saw the Chinese man walking out of the men's bathroom carrying a briefcase. "And Captain Mayfield followed that man out," she whispered.

"What?" Hawk asked.

"Oh, go ahead and tell him," Lidia caved in. "Better yet,

I will. Hawk, earlier, when Nikki and I were walking to the tea room, we saw that rude Chinese man walk out of a men's restroom. He was carrying a briefcase in his hand. Captain Mayfield walked out of the bathroom behind him."

"The Chinese man wasn't carrying a briefcase when we first saw him walk down the hallway," Nikki pointed out.

"And," Lidia sighed, "I saw our Chinese friend stick his head in this dining room a short while ago, spot Captain Mayfield, and then leave."

"How long ago?" Nikki asked.

"Shortly before this Mr. Lane walked in and gave Captain Mayfield the weather report," Lidia explained.

"There's Captain Mayfield," Herbert said in a hushed whisper. Picking up his fork, he took a bite of salmon and smiled in Captain Mayfield's direction. Captain Mayfield paid no mind to Herbert. He walked straight to his table, told his dinner guests that he had to return to the bridge, and excused himself.

Hawk began to stand up. As he did, the lights in the dining room went out. Darkness rolled across the room like a heavy swell filled with watery graves. Women began screaming. Out of instinct, Hawk bent down, lifted his pants leg, and snatched the gun attached to his right ankle out of its holster. Before he could stand up, the lights came on again. And there, lying dead in the middle of the dining room, lay Captain Mayfield's body. More screams erupted.

Nikki shot to her feet. "Hawk?"

Hawk, realizing that he was holding a gun in his hand and that people were staring at him, quickly grabbed his badge from the back pocket of his pants and stood up. "My name is Detective Daily," he called out and began waving his badge around in the air. "I need everyone to remain seated."

Lidia grabbed Herbert's hand. "Not a word," she begged him. "Please don't call Nikki a jinx."

Herbert simply picked up a glass of water and took a drink. "When this ship sinks, then I'll call her a jinx."

Hearing Herbert's remark hurt Nikki's feelings. Forcing her mind to stay focused, she remained at Hawk's side as he continued to reassure everyone that he was a cop. As the screams slowly began to settle down, she followed Hawk over to Captain Mayfield's body. "Look," she said, pointing at the man's neck.

Hawk nodded his head. Bending down, he examined a wooden dart lodged in Captain Mayfield's throat. The dart was two inches in length, thin but firm, made of bamboo. "A poison dart," Hawk told Nikki. Shaking his head, he looked over his shoulder toward the set of doors leading into the dining room. The doors were open. "Whoever killed Mayfield had an accomplice. Someone threw the lights while the other blew the dart."

Nikki looked at Hawk. "Hawk, I..."

"Did you pack your gun like I told you?"

Nikki nodded her head. "Yes," she said, lowering her eyes back down to Captain Mayfield's face. "Someone should go get the ship's doctor."

Hawk saw Brody run into the dining room, spot Captain Mayfield lying on the floor, and rush over. "What happened?"

"This man has been murdered," Hawk told Brody.

Standing up, he showed Brody his badge and then pointed at the dart sticking out of Captain Mayfield's neck. "Go get the ship's doctor."

"I...yes, of course, Detective," Brody said, staring down at Captain Mayfield with disturbed eyes. Hurrying away, he vanished out into the hallway.

"Well," Hawk said, "seems like we're in a real spot, Nikki."

Nikki didn't reply. In her mind, she studied every feature of the Chinese man. Then she studied the briefcase she saw the man carrying. Outside, the storm grew worse as the seas began to dig a watery grave for the doomed ship.

6

"She's with me," Hawk told a man resembling a scarecrow with stringy black hair.

The man, wearing a neat and crisp blue and white uniform, moved away from the door leading into the medical bay. Hawk motioned for Nikki to follow him. Nikki nodded, looked to her left at Lidia and Herbert, and asked them to stay out in the passageway. "You can count on that," Lidia promised.

Walking into a medium-sized room with a green and white linoleum floor, Nikki carefully absorbed the layout: White metal shelves holding medical supplies attached to the left and right walls, three medical beds were pushed up against the back wall, an examining bed sat in the middle of the room, a wooden desk sat under a white medical cabinet on the right wall. The medical bay, Nikki guessed, appeared normal—normal except for a dead body lying on the examining bed. "Well?" Hawk asked Dr. Carter Rowen.

Dr. Rowen looked at Brody. Brody was standing at the

wooden desk nibbling on his thumbnail. "Shouldn't you be getting us back to the home port?" Nikki asked him.

"I heard the conversation between you and Mayfield," Hawk told Brody in a stern tone. "So go turn this ship around and—"

"I can't," Brody interrupted Hawk in a desperate voice. "I can't even call the Captain's death into the mainland." Nikki watched Brody pull a piece of paper out of his pocket. "When I left the dining room, I went back to the bridge to call the doctor. My immediate goal was to turn the ship around and head home, but this note was taped to the bridge door."

Hawk took the note from Brody and read it. Shaking his head, he handed the note to Nikki. "He has to keep the ship on course and make contact with the Coast Guard or the mainland only when contacted."

"And I have to pretend everything is okay," Brody added.

"If you disobey," Nikki read the note, "more people will die." The killer states he has eyes everywhere.

Dr. Rowen didn't seem bothered by the note. Instead, he walked to the wooden desk, brushed Brody aside, opened the top right drawer, and brought out a bottle of brandy. "Lovely voyage," he said, opening the bottle. Nikki watched him take a long, hard swig. "Now," he said, putting the bottle of brandy back into the desk drawer and focusing on Captain Mayfield, "about our dear, distinguished captain here."

"What do you know about the dart?" Hawk asked as he

followed Dr. Rowen over to the examining table. Nikki, still holding onto the note, followed Hawk.

"Bamboo," Dr. Rowen answered Hawk, "with a very small needle attached to the tip. The tip of the needle was dipped in poison. What kind of poison I do not know, but," Dr. Rowen said, pointing to Captain Mayfield's body, "as you can see, whatever type of poison was used, it is very deadly."

"And the killer—or killers—probably have more of that poison," Nikki said worriedly.

Hawk nodded. "Makes me want to put a suit of armor on."

Nikki turned her attention away from Captain Mayfield and focused on Brody. "Mr. Lane, tell me about yourself. I don't mean to be pushy, but Detective Hawk heard Captain Mayfield mention a ship called the *Blue Pearl*."

Brody stiffened. Dr. Rowen folded his arms together and chuckled arrogantly. "Our dear Mr. Lane has a dark past," he said.

"Shut up," Brody warned Dr. Rowen.

"Or what?" Dr. Rowen chuckled again. "You see," he told Nikki, "Mr. Lane was once the captain of a very fine cruise ship called the *Blue Pearl*. The ship belonged to a company in China."

"China?" Nikki asked.

"Shut up, Rowen," Brody barked again. Hawk held up his hand and shook his head.

Dr. Rowen sneered at Brody. "Mr. Lane's wife is Chinese, didn't he tell you? Anyway, he began work on the beautiful *Blue Pearl*. Oh, but tragedy struck. On a very dark and stormy night, Mr. Lane ran the ship into a cargo ship. The *Blue Pearl* was severely damaged and began to sink. Luckily no soul perished. Afterward, Mr. Lane was tarred and feathered, so to speak, and his life as a sea captain was over."

"It was proven that the captain of that cargo ship was drunk," Brody said in a desperate voice, now that his secret was out. "We were caught on the outer edge of a typhoon. I was pulling the ship inland—the sea was unbearable. I didn't see the cargo ship. Suddenly, it appeared over a wave and crashed into the port side of the *Blue Pearl*."

"Oh, but it was also proven that you had a hint of whiskey on your breath, as well," Dr. Rowen added.

"That's not true. I never drank on duty," Brody yelled. Running his hands through his hair he began to pace around the medical bay. "It's true, I was once a drunk. I spent many years on the bottle. But then I met my wife, and she is a God-fearing woman. She changed me. I never went to church before, but we did, all the time."

"I believe you," Nikki promised Brody. Walking over to the man, she put her hand on his shoulder. "Your wife is sick, isn't she?"

"She has a rare blood disease. The medical treatments are costly. I knew Captain Mayfield from the old days. One day he called me out of the blue and offered me a job. Money was tight; my wife needed her medical treatments, so I accepted," Brody explained. "I moved my wife to Seattle and began working on this ship."

"Was Mayfield involved in any shady side-doing?" Hawk asked.

Brody tensed. "Detective Hawk, my job was to sail this ship. What Captain Mayfield did was his business. My only concern is my wife and a paycheck. This ship brings in good money—a lot of money has gone into making this ship what it is."

"But?" Nikki asked, reading Brody's facial expression. The man was withholding something.

Brody looked at Dr. Rowen. Dr. Rowen shrugged his shoulders. "Don't look at me. I only give out seasickness pills."

"Talk to me, Mr. Lane. Please," Hawk insisted.

Brody walked over to the wooden desk, sat down in a black chair, and placed his hands together. "Captain Mayfield was using this ship for something. I don't know what, and I never did. It's like I said, my main concern is for my wife and a paycheck," he confessed.

"Go on," Hawk told Brody.

"I've seen certain passengers on this ship...shady characters, as you cops would say. I never asked questions, though. But when I kept seeing the same repeat passengers, I became suspicious. So last month, I set up a hidden camera in Captain Mayfield's room. Boy, if he had caught me, he would have fed me to the sharks...but I have my wife to take care of, you understand. If Captain Mayfield was involved in a criminal activity, I couldn't take the chance of being connected with him."

"I understand," Hawk assured Brody.

Brody rotated his neck to release tension before he continued. "It's true, Captain Mayfield was involved in criminal activity. He was smuggling diamonds, guns, counterfeit money—but not drugs."

"And you caught this on the hidden camera?" Nikki asked.

Brody nodded his head. "I put the tape in a safety deposit box at my bank. You know, just in case Captain Mayfield tried to pull anything, I had a hidden card up my sleeve to play."

"While willfully breaking the law by not reporting the man to the authorities," Hawk added.

"Detective Hawk, do you have a sick wife?" Brody snapped. "Do you see your wife sick day in and day out? Do you see your wife so weak at times that she can't even make it to the bathroom on her own? Do you fight with a selfish insurance company that refuses to pay more than twenty percent of her medical bills? Do you, huh?"

"No," Hawk admitted.

"Well I do," Brody said, fighting back tears. "This company pays me good money, money that pays for my wife's medical treatments. So if I broke the law by not reporting the man who got me this job, then arrest me. But let me tell you something, Detective, when the life of your loved one is on the line, you do your job and keep your mouth shut!"

"Bravo," Doctor Rowen clapped.

"Shut your mouth," Brody warned in a voice that caused Dr. Rowen to immediately stop clapping. "My wife is home with a caretaker right now. My only concern is getting back to her. But if I dare turn this ship around or send out an SOS, more people might be killed. So tell me, what should I do, Detective?"

Hawk rubbed the back of his neck. Looking at Nikki, he nodded. "I gotta go find that Chinese fella, Nikki."

"His name is Lei Johnson. He's half-Chinese and half-American," Brody told Hawk and then disclosed the man's cabin number. "Listen to me, you can't go playing John Wayne, Detective. I'm acting captain of this ship now. You have no proof that Mr. Johnson is the person who killed Captain Mayfield."

"I'm only going to question the man," Hawk promised Brody. "In the meantime, you try to keep this bucket of bolts afloat."

"Detective," Brody said, "we have a severe storm chasing our tail, and we're not going to be able to outrun it. When the storm catches up to us, we're going to hit swells that will make the bravest man on earth wet his pants and—"

"Wait," Nikki said, "if the killer wants you to keep this ship on course, he must be aware of the danger, which means whatever cargo he has must be really important."

"Remember, the killer didn't work alone," Hawk told Nikki.

Nikki nodded. "Hawk, the briefcase Lidia and I saw this Mr. Johnson carrying when he walked out of the bathroom? That must be the cargo."

Brody stood up from the desk. "I'm going back to the bridge. The storm will be on us within the next couple of hours. After that, this ship is going to be fighting for its life. I'll do what I can to make sure we come out of this alive."

Hawk waited until Brody left the medical bay before speaking. "Dr. Rowen, you didn't like Mayfield, did you?"

"I despised the man," Dr. Rowen confessed, "but he's my half-brother, so what can I do? After I almost lost my medical license, he hired me on as ship doctor."

"How did you almost lose your medical license?" Nikki asked.

Dr. Rowen walked to the desk, pulled out the brandy, and took another swig. "I went into surgery drunker than a skunk, my dear lady."

"Come on," Hawk told Nikki, disgusted with Dr. Rowen.

7

Out in the hallway, Nikki glanced at the few employees standing about and then turned her attention to Lidia and Herbert. "You guys better get to your cabin and batten down the hatches, okay?" she whispered in Lidia's ear. "Mr. Lane can't turn the ship around because the killer said if he does, more people will die. This ship has to stay on course. The storm Mr. Lane is worried about will be on us in about two hours."

"Oh dear," Lidia whispered. Looking at Herbert, she sighed. "Okay, honey, we'll be in our cabin. Where are you going to be?"

"The Chinese man we saw is a Mr. Lei Johnson. Hawk and I are going to question him," Nikki whispered and then hugged Lidia. "We'll come to your cabin later."

"Hawk, I demand answers," Herbert stated, folding his arms together.

"So do I," Hawk told Herbert and patted the man on his

shoulder. "You guys better get to your cabin and stay put. We'll be by later. Let's go, Nikki."

With careful eyes, Nikki studied the employees still standing around. When she spotted the young girl who had given her a bottle of water in the lounge earlier, she paused, began to speak, decided not to, and walked past the girl. Fifteen minutes later, she and Hawk were standing in front of Mr. Johnson's cabin door. Hawk pulled out his gun and badge. "You knock," he told Nikki, moving her to the left side of the door as he moved to the right side.

Nikki braced herself, stuck out her right hand, and knocked on the cabin's wooden door three times. "Mr. Johnson," Hawk yelled, "this is Detective Daily. Please open up. I need to ask you some questions."

To Nikki's surprise, the cabin door slowly opened. Lei Johnson appeared, calm, collected, and intelligent. "Yes, Detective?" he asked in a cold voice. With patient eyes, he examined Hawk's badge.

"May we speak inside your cabin, please, sir?" Hawk asked.

"No," Lei answered, stepping out into the passageway. Pulling the cabin door shut behind him, he examined Nikki. The woman was lovely in every aspect, but dangerous. Her eyes held a brilliance that was difficult to understand.

"You are aware that Captain Mayfield is dead?" Hawk asked Lei.

Lei took his right hand and knocked a piece of lint off of his suit. "I heard rumors, yes," he answered. "Some low-paid servant on this ship informed me that Captain Mayfield had been killed by a poison dart."

"Yes," Nikki told Lei, easing over to Hawk. Lei Johnson looked like a man who took good care of himself, muscular and fit. The last thing she wanted was for him to strike out at her unexpectedly. "The dart was made of bamboo."

"I see," Lei said, narrowing his eyes. "And you, Detective Hawk, believe I am the killer?"

Hawk held his gun down at his side. He had enough distance to get off a single shot if Lei tried anything. "I'm not implying anything. But it has been brought to our attention you have made this same cruise a few times. Also, you were seen leaving a public bathroom earlier with Captain Mayfield."

Lei glanced at Nikki. He remembered seeing her in the hallway after leaving the bathroom. "Detective, I run a diamond business. My card."

While gripping his gun tighter, Hawk watched Lei reach into his jacket and retrieve a business card. Reaching out his left hand, he took the card. "Sea Diamonds," he read aloud.

"I sell diamonds to people on vacation. This ship, as you can see, is quite remarkable. Only the wealthy can afford passage, unlike those who purchase cheap tickets on those cheesy cruise ships that sail to overpriced tropical islands," Lei explained. "I made arrangements with Captain Mayfield to begin selling diamonds on this ship. I was in the bathroom with Captain Mayfield earlier. I went to the bathroom to retrieve my diamonds. Captain Mayfield was holding them in the ship's safe for me. I know a bathroom is an unlikely place, but one has to be careful."

"Why were you so rude on the dock earlier?" Nikki

demanded. "You walked right past my friend and were very rude."

"I have not been in a very pleasant mood, I'm afraid," Lei explained. "On the last voyage, it was brought to my attention that Captain Mayfield was smuggling diamonds, guns, and other items on this ship. It was also on the last voyage that Captain Mayfield threatened my life."

"How so?" Hawk demanded.

"He told me that I would begin smuggling his diamonds for him, or he would hold my diamonds in the ship's safe and not return them to me. I did as he ordered me to do. This morning, I returned to the ship to get my diamonds. Captain Mayfield gave them to me, only they were fakes. I was very angry. I have since calmed down."

"Why?" Nikki asked. "I believe you would be very upset."

"I was," Lei assured Nikki, "but my diamonds were returned to me about an hour and a half ago."

"They were?" Hawk asked.

Lei nodded. "I heard a knock at the cabin door. When I opened it, I saw a briefcase sitting out in the hall. The suitcase contained my diamonds."

Nikki gave Hawk a confused look. "About an hour and a half ago... Captain Mayfield was murdered about an hour ago."

"Mr. Johnson, a witness saw you enter the dining room, look at Captain Mayfield, and then leave. Shortly after, he was murdered. Can you explain your presence in the dining room?"

"I went to confront Captain Mayfield," Lei confessed. "I

wanted to accuse, insult, and embarrass the man in front of the passengers. I was furious. Then, at the last second, I decided that if I wanted my diamonds back, I needed a different approach. I left the dining room and ventured to Captain Mayfield's quarters. I entered his cabin and began searching for my diamonds."

"But to no avail," Nikki said.

Lei shook his head. "I'm afraid not. I returned here, to my own cabin, and began trying to conceive a plan. That's when the underpaid boy knocked on my door and told me there had been a murder. Shortly after, there was another knock on my door."

"The second knock on your door revealed your diamonds, is that right?" Hawk asked.

"Yes," Lei answered, allowing a smile to touch his lips. "I have examined each diamond, and they are authentic. I wish I could repay the good Samaritan who returned my diamonds, but I'm afraid that person remains anonymous."

"Mr. Johnson, remain in your cabin for the time being. If your diamonds are as valuable as you say they are, then you could become a target," Hawk told Lei. "Also, a very dangerous storm is about to trap this ship in open water, so it's gonna get rough. I need you to stay where I can find you. Go back in your cabin, lock the door, and stay put, okay?"

"Before you go," Nikki asked, "can you describe the person who told you Captain Mayfield had been murdered?"

Lei glared at Nikki with cold eyes. "The employees of this ship all look the same to me...it's the uniforms," he said.

Slithering back into his cabin, he closed the cabin door and locked it.

"He's lying," Nikki told Hawk as they walked away from the cabin door.

"Yep." Hawk shoved his gun down into a belt holster on his right hip. "Right now, Lei Johnson is our number one suspect."

8

Walking to the elevator, Nikki suddenly felt as if a huge rock struck the boat. The ship began to list dangerously to its starboard side. Unable to keep her balance, Nikki crashed into Hawk. Hawk threw out his hand, balanced himself against the right wall of the passageway, and quickly threw his left arm around Nikki's shoulder. "Whoa...settle down," he told the ship.

Certain the ship was about to capsize, Nikki closed her eyes and prepared for the worst. When the ship began to even out, she eased her eyes open, looked around, and let out her breath. "We need to get topside and see what hit the ship."

"A wave hit the ship," Hawk told Nikki. "Storm must have caught up to us earlier than they thought."

Hearing a few cabin doors open, Nikki looked down the hallway at scared faces. "It's okay," she called out, "I think a wave hit the ship. You should all get topside."

Hawk noticed Lei Johnson didn't open his cabin door. "Come on," he told Nikki, "we'll take the stairs."

Once topside, Nikki rushed to the bridge with Hawk. She stopped briefly and peered out a window. "My goodness, Hawk, will you look at that," she said, feeling the bow of the ship dip down and then pull up as it struggled through a deadly swell.

Hawk looked out the window at the storm. The sky was dark, but the emergency lights attached to the superstructure were able to cast a clear picture of what was taking place outside. Even though he couldn't see the waves, he could hear their power. The rain was falling as if a dam had exploded. Raging winds were screaming and howling like a group of lost soldiers determined to finish their battle in a time long forgotten; a battle that would never end in their hearts. "Even if the ship sank and everyone made it into the lifeboats, I don't see how that would help much," he told Nikki. "Pray, okay?"

"I have," Nikki promised.

Hearing the door to the bridge open, Nikki spotted Brody stepping out. "Mr. Lane," she called out.

Brody spotted Nikki and Hawk. Forcing a fake calmness to consume his face, he approached them. "I guess that storm caught up to us early?" Hawk asked.

"No," Brody corrected Hawk, "what we're witnessing now is a summer shower compared to what's coming. When the full force of the storm arrives, you'll know it."

"Where are you going?" Nikki asked Brody, trying to conceal her worry.

"To get a cup of coffee," Brody confessed. "Ms. Bates, I have a good man at the wheel. He'll keep us on course. As acting captain, it is my duty to check on the passengers. But first, I need a cup of coffee."

"We spoke to Lei Johnson," Hawk informed Brody. Feeling the bow of the ship dip forward again, Hawk reached out and grabbed Nikki. When the ship leveled out, Hawk explained the exchange he and Nikki shared with Lei Johnson. "I could have forced my way into his cabin, but my guess is if he is the killer, he wouldn't have the poison where anyone could easily locate it."

"It's clear Mr. Johnson isn't acting alone, Mr. Lane," Nikki told Brody. "He could be working with a crew member...or crew members, or a passenger. Or passengers. We don't know how many people are involved. However," Nikki paused, "my guess is he's being assisted by one or more crew members."

"Because of the lights?" Hawk asked.

Nikki nodded. "The lights in the dining room went off at a precise time and came on at a precise time. Mr. Lane, the young lady at the store counter in the passenger lobby, who is she? The name engraved on her name tag is Tara."

"Tara Farndale," Brody told Nikki, "age nineteen, high school drop-out, arrested for drug use at the age of seventeen, gets paid minimum wage to smile and be friendly to guests. I know about every single crew member on this ship, Ms. Bates. The owner of this ship likes to hire misfits...like myself, I guess you can say. He believes in giving people second chances. But Captain Mayfield did the actual hiring, and I fear he hired people who would do as he ordered them to."

"Have you ever met the owner?" Nikki asked.

"No," Brody replied. "The owner of this ship is a mystery to us all. Captain Mayfield was his front man. I really need a cup of coffee. When the storm hits I'll be at the wheel, and I don't want to face the storm with only hot tea in my system."

"We'll walk with you," Hawk told Brody.

Returning to the dining room, Nikki was relieved to see only crew members present. They were clearing plates and stacking chairs. Not a single one of them spoke to another. The mood was tense. Every face held a deep worry that clearly told Nikki she needed to worry, too. "Hey, Tara," Brody called to the young woman who had been attending to the guest lounge shop earlier in the morning, "three cups of coffee, please."

Tara looked at Nikki and Hawk for a few seconds, smiled politely, and walked off toward the kitchen with a broom in her hand. Sitting down at a table that had been stripped of its table cloth and dishes, Brody studied the faces of the crew members cleaning the dining room. "They know I can't turn the ship back," he told Nikki and Hawk. "Word gets around this ship in mysterious ways. Someone is always leaking private information."

"Dr. Rowen would be my guess in this case," Nikki said, sitting down across from Brody. Hawk chose to remain standing.

"Most likely," Brody agreed. Shaking his head, he called out to the crew members, "We're going to get through this, guys."

The young man who had taken Nikki's ticket earlier dropped a plate down onto the table he was clearing. His face was no longer friendly. "I didn't sign on to drown," he complained. "You have no right to risk our lives. Captain Mayfield—"

"Captain Mayfield is dead, and if I take this ship off course, more people can die," Brody barked at the young man.

"We might all die if you don't get us out of this storm," the young man barked back. "Man, this job is lame. I'm through. If we live through this, you can have my uniform and shove it."

"You can leave the dining room," Brody told the young man in a stern voice. "You are hereby terminated from your position. Go to your quarters and remain there."

"Fine with me," the young man said. Turning toward the other crew members, he asked: "Anyone else with me? Joe? Richard? Jennifer?"

A young woman with long, pretty black hair and a scared face shook her head. "There's a killer loose, Matt. I'm staying topside."

Other crew members echoed the young woman's words. "Suit yourself," Matt said and huffed away.

"I'm going to get us to port in one piece," Brody promised the crew members. "I know what you're all thinking—another storm, and good old Brody is at the wheel. But let me make this clear, the captain of that cargo ship that struck the *Blue Pearl* was drunk, and I was stone cold sober. Someone had to take the fall, and unfortunately, it ended up being me."

Spotting Tara carrying a tray holding three white coffee cups, Nikki patted Brody's arm. "Here comes the coffee."

Brody sighed miserably. "Yeah," he said, lowering his eyes to his hands.

Hawk put his hand on Brody's shoulder. "When a man is bound and determined to redeem himself, he will in time. Trying to prove yourself to a bunch of young kids is only going to cause you a headache."

"Here's the coffee, Mr. Lane," Tara said. Carefully, she placed the coffee tray down on the table. "I brought out some sugar and half-and-half."

"Thanks," Brody said.

Tara smiled at Nikki and Hawk and went back to sweeping. "Sweet girl," Nikki said, taking a cup of coffee and lifting it up to Hawk. Hawk gratefully took the cup of coffee from Nikki. She handed the second cup to Brody. "Did you order the passengers to their cabins?"

"Yeah," Brody said, taking the cup of coffee from Nikki. "When the full force of the storm arrives, I'm going to need everyone in their cabins. If the time comes, I'll give the order to abandon ship. Captain Mayfield was going to walk all the passengers through the emergency procedures once the weather cleared. I wish he had waited to depart from the port after the storm passed, but he was anxious to get out to sea."

Hawk sipped his coffee. With steady eyes, he studied each and every crew member working in the dining room. "Mr. Lane, any idea who might be helping the killer?" he said loudly enough to cause most of the crew members to stop working and look over at him. Looking at Nikki, he nodded.

Nikki quickly caught onto Hawk's plan. "Yes," she said, making sure her voice was loud enough to be heard across the dining room, "we're certain it's one of the passengers that is assisting the killer."

Brody gave Nikki a confused look. "But you said—"

"We're certain it's one of the passengers," Nikki interrupted him.

"Uh, I can get you the list of all the passengers' names," Brody replied.

"Please do," Nikki said, picking up her cup of coffee. Before she could take a sip, Tara eased her way out of the dining room and back into the kitchen. Nikki felt her heart break. "There goes the rat to the cheese," she told Hawk miserably.

"Let's cut her off at the pass," Hawk told Nikki, putting down his coffee. "Mr. Lane, we'll meet you back at the bridge in a few minutes."

Standing up, Nikki took a sip of hot coffee and shook her head. "She was so sweet, too," she said.

"Come on," Hawk told Nikki, taking her hand. Without

wasting another second, he hurried Nikki out of the dining room and jogged to the staircase. "We don't want to frighten her," he said, stepping into a wooden stairwell lit with bright lights. "Let her get to Johnson's door and see what happens."

9

Feeling a hard wave strike the ship, Nikki nearly lost her balance. Grabbing the wooden railing attached to the stairwell, she shook her head. "Hawk, I'm not that great a swimmer," she confessed.

"Me neither," Hawk told her, waiting for the ship to balance out. "You can use me as a life jacket if you want."

"You big lug," Nikki said, feeling a smile break through her worry like a single ray of sunshine.

"Careful now," Hawk said as he began to walk down the stairs, "or I may arrest you for insulting an officer of the law."

Nikki took her left hand and playfully slapped Hawk in the back of the head. "Add assault to my charge list."

"Will do," Hawk said as he reached the deck Lei Johnson's cabin was located on. He carefully eased open a heavy wooden door, peeked out into the passageway, and smiled. "There she goes, heading straight for Johnson's cabin."

Nikki ducked under Hawk's arm and peered out into the hallway. With a broken heart, she watched Tara stop at Lei Johnson's cabin door, nervously scan the hallway, and then knock on the door. "Why would she tell me Johnson was on a previous cruise?" Nikki whispered to herself.

Seconds later, Lei Johnson opened the door, stuck his head out, examined the empty hallway, and then yanked Tara inside before she could react. "Let's go," Hawk said, pulling out his gun. On swift feet, he exploded out of the stairwell, charged up to the cabin door, raised his right leg, and with one hard foot, kicked open the door with his gun at the ready. "Freeze!" he yelled, spotting Lei Johnson holding Tara by her right wrist.

Tara wasn't the only one in Lei Johnson's cabin. The young man whom Brody had fired in the dining room was also present, standing next to a porthole, looking out at the storm. "It's not what you think," Tara told Hawk. When she saw Nikki appear, she yanked away from Lei Johnson and ran to Matt. Matt quickly put his arm around Tara's shoulder and pulled her close.

"Stand still," Hawk warned Lei, still holding his gun at the ready. "One move and you're a dead man, are we clear?"

"The heroic cop," Lei replied in a disgusted voice. "You make me sick. You break down the door and charge into my cabin, ready to assume the worst of me. What evidence do you have against me?"

"We saw you grab Tara," Nikki said, standing in the doorway.

"You both know the cargo I have in my cabin. Yes, I

me in the kitchen when the lights went off. I had just closed down my station in the passenger lounge and wanted to help Matt in the kitchen."

"There are plenty of witnesses, smart guy," Matt snapped at Hawk. "I was filling bowls with butterscotch pudding."

Hawk bit down on his lower lip. "Someone killed the lights. My gut tells me if it wasn't you, then you know who it was. Talk to me, boy."

"Talk to my lawyer," Matt told Hawk. "I plead the right to, you know, cop, remain silent."

"I do the same," Lei told Hawk. Walking to a twin bed in the cabin, Lei sat down at the foot, folded his right leg on his left knee, and stared at Hawk. Hawk didn't care. He lowered his gun, snatched a pair of handcuffs from his front pocket, and walked over to Matt. Before Matt could object, Hawk popped one handcuff onto his left wrist, pulled him over to the bed, and slapped the other cuff down onto Lei's right wrist. "Don't move an inch," Hawk told Lei, keeping his gun at the ready as he slapped the handcuff onto his wrist.

"What is this all about?" Lei demanded.

Hawk ordered Tara to leave the cabin. "As of now, you two are my main suspects. Until that changes, you will remain in this cabin, handcuffed together. I am posting an armed guard outside of the cabin door. If you try and open it, that guard will have my full permission to shoot you. Are we clear?"

"I'll have your job," Lei threatened Hawk.

"Nah," Hawk grinned. "Now where are your diamonds?"

"No," Lei yelled.

"I am putting your diamonds in the ship's safe for now. You will get them back if you are proven innocent."

Lei drew in an angry breath. "I have hidden my diamonds in a location that no one will find," he promised Hawk. "Search my cabin; the diamonds are not here."

"Fine," Hawk said in a simple voice, "if this ship sinks, your diamonds will sink with it. Think on that. But you don't care, do you? You left a note threatening to murder more people if Mr. Lane took this ship off course."

Lei's face went pale. He began to speak but quickly looked down at the handcuff on his wrist and said nothing. "You'll pay for this," Matt promised Hawk. "Tara and I deserve to get married, you idiot, but you don't care, do you? You don't care about what she's been through, do you? You don't care that—"

"Shut up and listen to me," Hawk told Matt. "Right now, all I care about is getting you two into a jail. And if by some chance you aren't the killer, Mr. Johnson, then all I care about is finding the real killer. But I think you are the killer."

Nikki pulled Tara out into the hallway. "Honey, please," she begged, "are you really telling the truth? Were you in the kitchen with Matt when the lights went off?"

"Yes," Tara promised. "I wouldn't lie about a thing like

that. Matt was making pudding bowls. I was standing right next to him. When we heard the passengers begin to scream when the lights came back on, we ran out of the kitchen. That's when we saw Captain Mayfield lying dead on the floor. Honest."

"Okay," Nikki said in a soothing voice, "but for now, I'm afraid you have to be confined to your quarters, okay? Detective Daily and I will escort you."

"I understand, I guess," Tara said in an upset voice. "What is going to happen to Matt? Please, he can't go to jail. He was only doing this for me, you know?"

Nikki nodded her head. "If Matt is innocent, he'll go free. If he's guilty, he'll answer to a court of law," she told Tara, watching Hawk close the cabin door and step out into the hallway.

"Well," Hawk said, "I think we caught our killer and his accomplice."

"No," Tara shook her head. "We told you, Matt was in the kitchen making pudding bowls when the lights went off."

Before Hawk could reply, Nikki heard the door to the stairwell click shut. "Hawk, someone is in the stairwell!"

Hawk looked down the hallway and took off running. Nikki grabbed Tara's hand and followed Hawk. Reaching the stairwell, Hawk burst in with his gun ready. Looking upward, he caught a glimpse of someone exiting the stairwell onto the deck above. Giving chase, Hawk raced up the stairs. Nikki chased after Hawk, pulling Tara with her. Storming out of the stairwell onto the passenger deck where their own cabins were located, Hawk looked to his left and then to his right. "No one," he said, breathing hard. "Whoever it was is gone."

Nikki ran out of the stairwell. Looking to her left and then to her right, she saw only empty space. "The elevator is running. Whoever it was is in one of the rooms."

"It's no good," Hawk told Nikki. "It'll take all night to search each cabin. By then this ship could be at the bottom of the sea. Come on, let's get this girl to her quarters and then get back to the bridge. But first, let me go talk to Herbert."

Knowing that Hawk was right, Nikki examined the empty passageway once more. Maybe, she thought, Mr. Lei Johnson might not be the killer after all.

10

After locking Tara in her quarters, Hawk and Nikki hurried back to the bridge. Brody was standing outside in the hallway, waiting for them. "Matt called me from Mr. Johnson's room. He told me you handcuffed him to Mr. Johnson. Is that true?"

"Yep," Hawk said, proud of himself.

"We saw Tara leave the dining room. We found her knocking on Mr. Johnson's cabin door. Matt was inside," Nikki explained. "Mr. Lane, you have to admit, that is very suspicious."

"I guess it is," Brody admitted.

Hawk explained about Matt returning the diamonds to Lei Johnson after Captain Mayfield's murder and then requesting reward money. "At first, I thought the boy was lying, and I made him believe I thought he was lying."

"Matt was telling the truth?" Brody asked.

Hawk shrugged his shoulders. "Mr. Lane, right now, I

have two people handcuffed together, and I have an armed guard standing outside in the hallway ready to shoot them if they try and leave. I actually have old Herbert standing guard. I gave him a gun. He'll shoot at anything, so be careful if you go down there."

"His wife, Lidia, is with him. She has my gun," Nikki told Brody. "We owe them big time, Hawk."

"Yeah, I know," Hawk agreed. Shaking his head, he peered out of a window into the storm. "Ship is really taking a hit."

"The full force of the storm is almost on us," Brody explained. "I...have just enough time to push this ship west and out of the direct path of the storm."

"No," Hawk said, "we have to stay on course. If Johnson isn't the killer, then we still have a real problem on our hands."

"Then who is the killer?" Brody asked, feeling the ship ride up a huge swell. "Forget my question. I have to return to the wheel. I'll keep us on course as long as possible."

Nikki watched Brody open the door to the bridge and run inside. "Who is the killer?" she asked Hawk. "I think we both know Mr. Johnson isn't the killer, Hawk. It seems like Captain Mayfield was strong-arming a lot of people, people who might have wanted him dead."

Hawk balanced himself against the passageway wall. He began to answer Nikki but caught a glimpse of an approaching person. Pulling out his gun, he saw Dr. Rowen jogging up to him. "Detective," Dr. Rowen yelled in an urgent voice, "Detective Daily, I—" Dr. Rowen suddenly stopped jogging. With an agonizing cry, he grabbed his neck, and then he dropped dead.

Hawk ran up to Dr. Rowen's body. "Look...another dart," he told Nikki.

Nikki leaned down next to Hawk, fully aware they were easy targets. With nervous eyes, she examined the bamboo dart lodged in Dr. Rowen's neck. "He's dead, Hawk," she said.

Hawk shot to his feet. "Stay right here," he ordered Nikki and ran off down the hallway, fighting to keep his balance as the ship fought its way through the storm.

"What were you going to tell Hawk?" Nikki asked Dr. Rowen, hugging her shoulders with shaking hands. After a few seconds, she drew up enough courage to lean back down and examine Dr. Rowen's pockets. And there, in the dead man's front pocket, she found a crinkled-up piece of paper with someone's handwriting on it. She grabbed some latex gloves from her pocket. *Never leave home without them,* she thought, as she put them on. "Oh dear," Nikki said, recognizing the handwriting on the piece of paper.

Standing up, she backed away from Dr. Rowen's body until her back was pressed up against the door leading into the bridge. Using her left hand, she reached down into the front pocket of her dress and drew out the letter the killer had left taped to the bridge door. Comparing the letter to the piece of crinkled-up paper she found on Dr. Rowen's body, Nikki was able to clearly see the handwriting on both pieces of paper. "The handwriting matches," she said. Wishing Hawk was with her, Nikki looked down the hallway as the ship struggled over another large swell. Barely able to keep her balance, Nikki began to feel fatigue set in. "No time for sleeping," she told herself, thinking of her warm bed back in her cabin.

A few minutes later, Hawk appeared. "No good," he said out of breath. "I lost him."

"Look," Nikki said, showing Hawk the piece of paper she had retrieved from Dr. Rowen's body and then the note the killer had taped to the bridge door. "Hawk, the handwriting matches."

"Seasick pills ordered," Hawk read from the crinkled-up piece of paper.

"Hawk, the killer is a crew member," Nikki said. "We need to ask Mr. Lane who orders the medical supplies for Dr. Rowen."

Hawk agreed. With a hard fist, he banged on the bridge door. Brody opened the door with impatient hands. "I don't have time to speak with you—"

Hawk tossed a thumb over his shoulder at Dr. Rowen's body. "Dr. Rowen has been murdered," he interrupted Brody. "The killer was just in this passageway."

Brody froze. Unable to speak, he stared at Dr. Rowen's body. "Mr. Lane, who orders the medical supplies for Dr. Rowen?"

"I...uh..." Brody attempted to speak. Forcing his mind to think, he eased around his shock and answered Nikki. "The home office. Dr. Rowen makes a list of what he needs after each cruise and drops it off at the home office."

"You didn't recognize the writing on the letter the killer left on this door, did you?" Nikki asked.

Brody shook his head. "No."

Hawk showed Brody the wrinkled-up piece of paper Nikki found in Dr. Rowen's pocket. "The handwriting matches," he said, showing Brody the killer's letter.

Brody examined each piece of paper with nervous eyes. "I don't recognize the handwriting, I'm sorry. But it does appear the handwriting on both pieces of paper matches."

"Mr. Lane, do you have a pen?" Nikki asked. Brody took a pen out of his jacket pocket and handed the pen to Nikki. Nikki put an X on both pieces of paper and handed the pen back to Brody. "Thank you."

"Sure," Brody replied as he tilted his head and wrinkled his brow.

Nikki took the killer's letter and the piece of paper she found on Dr. Rowen and shoved them down into the front pocket of her dress. "We need to get his body to the medical bay."

"I understand," Brody said as a huge wave bashed up against the ship, sending water racing over the bow, temporarily submerging it completely. "I have to get back to the wheel."

"Go on," Hawk said, shaking his head. "You handle keeping us above water, and we'll handle the rest." Brody nodded and hurried back into the bridge. "Nikki?"

"Yes?" Nikki asked, fighting to keep her balance.

"How did Dr. Rowen know we were up here?"

Nikki considered Hawk's question. “The killer,” she answered as the truth struck her mind like a powerful wave crashing down. “Hawk, Dr. Rowen was led here.”

“But why?” Hawk asked. “The killer could have put that poison dart in Dr. Rowen's neck anyplace.”

course for some dangerous reason. I'm inclined to believe the killer might want this ship to sink."

Hawk stared into Nikki's beautiful eyes. "For insurance money?"

Nikki nodded. "It's possible."

"But the killer would go down with the ship?" Hawk asked, confused.

"Would he?" Nikki asked as alarm bells went off in her head. "Hawk, would he? What if there is a bomb on this ship set to go off at a certain time? The killer can jump ship and set the bomb off by remote control."

Hawk bit down on his lower lip. "The killer knocked off Captain Mayfield...but why? Maybe because Mayfield knew too much or crossed a line? The killer then took out Dr. Rowen as a message for me to back off, but Dr. Rowen seemed awful anxious to tell me something, didn't he?"

"Yes," Nikki agreed.

"Okay, Nikki, let's go through the process of elimination. We'll start checking this ship for a bomb."

"What about the killer?" Nikki worried.

Hawk bit down on his lower lip again. Shaking his head, he walked over to Dr. Rowen's desk and pulled out the bottle of Brandy. "Well, Dr. Rowen, you old boozehound, you had an awful end and—" Hawk stopped talking.

"What?" Nikki asked, alarmed.

"Look," he said, handing her the bottle of brandy. Staring at the bottle, he pointed to a plastic bag holding a note. "We have a message."

Nikki ran to the cleaning station sink, emptied the bottle

of brandy and pulled the plastic bag free. Handing Hawk the empty brandy bottle, she nervously glanced around the empty medical bay, expecting the killer to somehow materialize out of thin air. She waited until the ship fought through a thunderous swell, and then pulled the message out of the plastic bag. "The ship is doomed. Get off it while you still can. BOOM," Nikki read the message aloud to Hawk and then grew silent as all the color drained from her face. "It is a bomb," she whispered, terrified.

"A bomb... Maybe the killer didn't take out Dr. Rowen as a warning to me after all," Hawk told Nikki, shaking his head. Rubbing the back of his neck, he began to pace around the medical bay. Having a dead body lying on a bed in the middle of the bay made Hawk feel uneasy. The dead body could have been himself, or even worse, Nikki. "Nikki, it's too late to turn around. We're stuck in this storm for good. So the killer wants to sink this ship in the storm, collect the insurance money, and walk away free as a bird. It's a good plan, too. The killer can blame the storm for sinking the ship, and who would be able to say otherwise? All the witnesses will be dead."

Nikki began biting on her thumbnail. Feeling like a mouse caught in an impossible maze, she watched Hawk pace around. "Hawk, if Mr. Johnson and Matt aren't the team we're looking for, that means the killer's accomplice is still loose on this ship. The more I think about it, the more I believe that Mr. Johnson isn't the killer. Yes, the man fits the role, and I'm sure he has some skeletons in his closet. But I don't think he killed Captain Mayfield or Dr. Rowen."

"I'm listening."

"Hawk, Matt took Mr. Johnson his diamonds after Captain Mayfield was killed. Why would Mr. Johnson kill Captain Mayfield before retrieving his diamonds? That would be like killing a man who owed you money. You would never collect," Nikki explained.

Hawk considered Nikki's explanation. It made sense to him. "Yeah, he's also handcuffed to Matt in his cabin. There's no way he could have killed Dr. Rowen, either."

"Which leaves us back at square one," Nikki sighed miserably. "We have a killer on the loose and someone—or a group of people—helping him. I'm just wondering how Dr. Rowen came to find out the ship is doomed."

"Maybe he had a little chat with the killer," Hawk attempted to joke.

Nikki froze. "Hawk, that's not so far-fetched," she said. "Maybe Dr. Rowen knew the killer all along? Maybe—come on!" Nikki grabbed Hawk's hand and dashed out of the medical bay. Taking a dangerous chance of throwing her body into the open where a poison dart could easily come flying at her from any direction and take her life, she ran toward the stairwell and made her way back to Tara's quarters.

12

"What are we doing back here?" Hawk asked, catching his breath.

"You'll see," Nikki said, knocking on the door. A few seconds later, Tara opened the door with tears in her eyes. "Oh, it's you, Ms. Bates and Detective Daily. I was hoping it was Matt."

"Tara," Nikki said quickly, "when you were in the kitchen before the lights went out, did you happen to see Dr. Rowen?"

"Dr. Rowen?" Tara asked, wiping at her tears. "Let me think..." Tara pushed her mind back into the kitchen. "It was really busy. The cooks were talking and laughing, people were taking orders out to the front tables. Matt was filling the pudding bowls, and we were talking about getting our apartment. I was really excited."

"Keep going," Nikki told Tara in a patient voice. She had been Tara's age once, too, and understood how the mind of a nineteen-year-old girl operated.

"Well, Matt and I were talking about saving money for the security deposit, and the lights went off," Tara explained, straining her memory. "I...wait," she exclaimed. "Ms. Bates, Detective Daily, I did see Dr. Rowen in the kitchen. He was standing near the walk-in cooler, eating a chocolate, as a matter of fact. He was talking to a cook. I really didn't think much of it. I mean, it was dinner time."

"And the switches that control the dining room and kitchen lights?" Hawk asked.

Tara looked at Hawk. "Detective Daily, the main control panel is located in the kitchen." Tara stopped. Her eyes grew wide. "Near the walk-in cooler."

"Bingo," Hawk told Nikki. "We've found the killer's accomplice. Nikki, remind me to put a ring on your finger and sweep you away to a romantic island someday."

Nikki smiled. "I'll settle for making sea salt chocolates together in my kitchen," she told Hawk. "Okay, Tara, you've been a great help. Now I have a job for you and Matt. A very important job. Come with me."

Hawk gave Nikki a confused look but trusted in her plan. Taking out his gun, he followed Nikki and Tara back to Lei Johnson's cabin, Nikki immediately hugged Lidia, who was standing guard there with Herbert. "We believe there is a bomb on the ship," she explained in a low voice.

"A bomb!" Herbert yelled.

Lidia slapped Herbert across the chest. "Can you say it

any louder?" she fussed. "Quiet down, you big oaf. Nikki, what makes you think there's a bomb on the ship?"

The word 'bomb' caused Tara to fall into panic mode. She ran for Lei's cabin door. Hawk grabbed her. "Whoa, girl, not so fast. You can't go broadcasting what you're hearing."

"But a bomb!" Tara said, panicked. "We have to get off this ship."

"Tara," Hawk said in a stern tone, "if you abandoned ship on one of those flimsy lifeboats attached up on the main deck, the sea would swallow you whole."

Tara knew Hawk was right. What chance did a small wooden lifeboat have against the raging storm outside? "What do we do?" she begged.

Nikki put her hand on Tara's shoulder. Soothingly, she spoke in a low and caring voice. "Tara, I need you and Matt to locate the bomb. I know that Matt knows this ship inside and out."

"Wait a minute," Hawk objected. "I'm not so sure I want to trust Matt, Nikki. He may try to jump ship with this girl."

"I won't let him do anything stupid, I promise," Tara told Hawk in a shaky voice.

Herbert huffed. Lowering the gun in his hand, he glared at Nikki. "Next time I'm staying home."

"Oh, be quiet," Lidia griped at Herbert. "How could Nikki or Hawk know any of this was going to happen? For crying out loud, it's not like they planned this, Herbert."

Herbert eyed Nikki with distaste. "It seems to me that trouble fits this woman like an old shoe. Lidia, when we get home—if we get home—I forbid you to continue being friends with her. Do I make myself clear?"

Lidia looked at Herbert. Shaking her head in anger, she pointed her finger at his nose. "You listen to me, Herbert, I love you. I enjoy our life together. But if you dare, and I mean dare, try to break up the bond Nikki and I have created with one another, I'll leave you. Do you hear me?"

Shocked, Nikki began to interject. "Lidia, I don't mean to cause problems and—"

Lidia held up her hand at Nikki. Focused on Herbert, she continued. "All you have been doing this entire time is complaining about Nikki. I'm sick of it, do you hear me? Is it her fault a bomb is on this ship? But thank goodness she had the guts to find out. All you've been doing is fussing about how she has ruined your precious good time. Did she kill Captain Mayfield with a poison dart, you old windbag?"

Hawk eased Tara back. The argument was escalating, and it was better to stand clear. Herbert said, "Lidia, you've never spoken to me like this before. Can't you see that I am concerned about—"

"Concerned, my foot," Lidia huffed. "Anything that disturbs your quiet life at the campground you mark as hostile. For crying out loud, Herbert, Nikki and Hawk have solved three murder cases in our town. How is that wrong?"

"Need I remind you she almost cost you your life?" Herbert huffed back at Lidia.

"I risk my life every day I go into town, Herbert. Not every tourist who comes into the chocolate store is an angel, you know. Anybody could walk into the store and shoot me dead," Lidia pointed out. "Herbert, I promise, if you don't stop clawing at Nikki, I will leave you. Not because I want to, but because you are wrong. You're attacking an innocent woman, and I can't stand for that. I expect better from you, and right now I am downright ashamed to be your wife."

"Lidia!" Herbert gasped. "I...I..." he stuttered. Slowly, he looked at Nikki. That's when he realized that, yes, it was true. He was attacking Nikki because this strange woman who had shaken up his entire life scared him. It was one thing to risk her own life chasing deadly criminals, but it was another thing to risk the life of his wife. "I resent you because you placed Lidia's life in danger. You have no right to involve people in your crazy schemes," Herbert snapped at Nikki. "Our life was fine without you." Without saying another word, he shoved the gun in his hand at Hawk. "Take this awful thing. I'm through being your watchdog."

Hawk took the gun. Herbert turned to Lidia and told her if she wanted to leave him, that was fine by him, and then he stormed off. "Oh dear," Lidia said. "Nikki, I better go talk to him."

"Hurry," Nikki pleaded and took the gun Lidia was holding. "I'm so sorry! I didn't mean to...oh, Lidia, can you ever forgive me?"

"This isn't your fault," Lidia promised.

Nikki watched Lidia chase after Herbert. "I've destroyed a marriage," she told Hawk in a pained voice.

"No, you didn't," Hawk said, shoving the gun Herbert gave him down into the front of his belt. "I can understand Herbert's anger. If I were in his shoes, I'd feel the same about you. He loves his wife, Nikki, and he's afraid to lose her. He's not blaming you for what's happening, but he needs to vent his anger at someone."

Nikki lowered her eyes and studied the gun she was holding. It felt like a poisonous snake in her hands. Growing quiet, she thought back to the tears she'd cried over Hawk in the medical bay. If she lost Hawk, her world would come to an end. And if Hawk was friends with a man who was constantly putting his life in danger, what would she do? "I would react the same way Herbert is reacting," she whispered. "Tara, go back to your room, honey. I'm not putting your life in danger. Detective Daily and I will search for the bomb."

13

Tara hesitated. Looking at the closed cabin door Matt was behind, she thought about the life they had planned together. "It's not fair," she told Nikki. "All Matt and I want to do is get married and love each other. Why do things like this keep happening?"

"Honey, go back to your cabin and—"

"No," Tara told Nikki, feeling anger rise up in her chest. "Ms. Bates, Detective Daily, you two are not familiar with this ship the way Matt is. If anyone can find a bomb, it's him. Please, let us try. I'm being very selfish because I'm only thinking of Matt and the life I want to share with him."

Hawk eased back to Lei Johnson's cabin door, took out a key from his pocket, and unlocked it. "Matt, Johnson, get out here," he ordered.

Lei Johnson and Matt appeared like two wet hornets. Matt stared at Hawk with eyes that could have melted hot iron. "What is it?" he demanded.

Using his left hand while holding his gun in his right,

Hawk fished the handcuff key out of his front pocket, tossed it to Tara, and told her to unlock Matt from Lei. "Listen to me," he explained in a tough voice, "we believe there is a bomb on this ship. Matt, we need you to find that bomb. If you don't, son, we're all dead."

Lei's face went white. His anger was instantly replaced with fear. "My diamonds," he whispered.

Hawk nodded his head. "Your diamonds will soon be at the bottom of the sea if that bomb isn't found. We believe the killer is the man who owns this ship."

"Mr. Fench?" Matt asked. "No way, that old coot is wheelchair-bound. I'd put my money on his son, though. Thorn Fench is a crummy guy. He thinks just because he rides around in a fancy Porsche and lives off his daddy's money he's better than anyone else."

Nikki looked at Hawk and then back at Matt. The ship was really struggling against the storm, causing everyone to struggle for balance at times. If a bomb was going to go off, it would be soon, before the ship managed to fight its way through the deadly sea. "Matt, did you ever see Captain Mayfield and this Thorn Fench together?"

"Oh sure," Matt said, watching Tara take the handcuffs off his wrist, "those two were real chummy."

"What does this guy look like?" Hawk asked.

Matt rubbed his wrist. "He's around your age, I guess...wavy blond hair, athletic-looking, the kind of guy that talks lies to the ladies, you know."

"What else?" Nikki pressed Matt. "Please, any detail, no matter how small, could be very helpful."

Matt watched Lei try to ease back into his cabin. Hawk

grabbed him and shook his head. Lei, tempted to put Hawk down to the floor with a single, skilled martial arts move, hesitated. Hawk was holding a gun, and Lei knew he would not hesitate to use it. Besides, Lei thought, what was the point of making matters worse? Even if he did escape and retrieve his diamonds, where could he run to? Like everyone else, he was trapped. His only chance of survival was to assist Hawk. "How can I be of assistance?" he asked, caving in.

Nikki handed Matt her gun. Hawk began to object, but Nikki shook her head at him. "Protect Tara and go find that bomb."

"You trust me?" Matt asked in a cynical voice, taking the gun from Nikki. "Lady, I could vanish so easily on this ship, and you and Tarzan over there would never find me."

"Don't," Tara told Matt in a desperate voice. Softly touching his face, she pulled his eyes to her. "Matt, you're better than this. We all are. People's lives are at stake—*our* lives are at stake. Please, don't be a jerk. Be the guy I've fallen in love with. Be my hero."

Matt stared into Tara's pleading eyes. He felt something stir deep inside his chest. "Okay," he promised Tara. Looking at Hawk, he steadied his attitude. "Detective, what do I do if I find the bomb? Can you disarm it?"

"I've had a little training," Hawk told Matt. "Son, all I can promise is that I'll do what I can."

"That doesn't make me feel better," Matt confessed. Shaking his head, he grabbed Tara's left hand. "Okay, I'll find that bomb. If we're gonna die, we might as well die trying to be heroes."

"Be careful," Nikki begged Matt. "I want to come to your wedding someday, okay?"

Matt nodded. "I'll be down in the engine room."

"Wait...wait a minute!" Lei called out. Against his better judgment, he made a confession: "I can disarm a bomb. I have training."

"Where?" Hawk asked.

"My secret," Lei replied. "I will go with Romeo and Juliet."

Hawk hesitated. "Okay," he said, giving in, "but if you try anything—"

"Detective," Lei said, "what would I try? Where can I run? Enough with the tough cop act, already. You do your job, and I'll do mine."

Hawk grabbed Lei by his jacket. "I'm not putting on an act. My main concern is for the lives of everyone on this ship. You may not have a conscience, but I do. Now get moving." Hawk shoved Lei toward Matt and Tara.

"I too once had a conscience," Lei told Hawk, "but life took that away. Another time, Detective, when the odds are even."

"Anytime," Hawk promised.

Nikki watched Matt, Tara, and Lei walk to the stairwell and disappear. "I hope that young man holds to his word," she told Hawk.

"In life," Hawk replied, "you work with what tools you have in the old toolbox. The question now is, what do we do?"

"Go inform Mr. Lane about the bomb," Nikki told Hawk. "After that, go back to my cabin and wait."

Something in Nikki's voice struck Hawk as strange. Nikki had a plan, a plan she didn't want prying ears to hear. It occurred to him that she was manipulating the killer. As scary as it was to realize that the killer was close by, hidden in some shadow, listening to every word being spoken, Hawk found himself grateful as well. "All we can do is wait and hope that boy finds the bomb," Hawk told Nikki.

Taking Hawk's hand, Nikki nodded up toward the ceiling. "Let's go see Mr. Lane."

14

Hawk knocked on the bridge door. The storm had now fully enveloped the ship. Thunderous waves, screaming winds, and pouring rain hollered above the dark sea with razor-sharp teeth. "Mr. Lane," Nikki yelled, "it's Ms. Bates and Detective Daily. We need to speak with you. It's urgent."

The bridge door opened up. Brody appeared. "What is it?" he asked in a voice that told Nikki and Hawk the ship was in real danger.

"We believe there is a bomb on the ship, and the killer will detonate it before the ship is able to escape this storm," Nikki explained quickly. "Mr. Lane, how much longer will this storm hold us captive?"

Brody's face went pale. "Uh, hard to tell, the system is massive. Even if I wanted to push the ship west, I couldn't. We're trapped."

Feeling the bow of the ship dip dangerously forward,

Nikki flung her arms out for balance and managed to grab onto Hawk. "Okay," Nikki told Brody, "Detective Daily and I will be in my cabin. It's too dangerous to be out anymore."

"Are we going to sink?" Hawk asked Brody, reading the man's worried face.

"Engine room is reporting minor flooding," Brody confessed. "The hull of this ship is old, Detective. As you can feel, we're being knocked around like peas in a can. We've been knocked off course, and there is nothing I can do about it, I'm afraid."

"Do your best," Nikki told Brody. "We'll be in my cabin. All we ask is that you send some men out to find the bomb, okay? There's nothing else we can do."

Nikki stuck out her hand to shake Brody's. Brody, without thinking, shook Nikki's hand. "I'll do what I can, but the chances may be slim," he replied in a calm voice. Returning to the bridge, Brody closed the wooden door behind him.

Nikki quickly gave Hawk a look that told him not to ask any questions. "Come on, let's get to my cabin and wait," she told him.

Hawk stared at the door leading into the bridge. His gut began to nibble at him. What did Nikki know that he didn't? Fighting to stand upright as a wave crashed against the port side of the ship, rocking it violently, Hawk knew that whatever Nikki knew, she would soon reveal it to him.

On the bridge, Brody ordered an officer named John Brownfield to keep the ship heading due north at all costs. "We have a killer loose. Try and keep on course no matter what. It's prudent we do as the killer has ordered."

"I'll do my best, Lane," the man replied, fighting to keep the ship on its set course.

"I'll be back in two hours. I have to go check on the passengers and then see how much water the engine room is taking on."

"I understand. I'll hold her steady."

Brody nodded, walked to the back wall, and exited the bridge through a private hallway.

"Hawk," Nikki said, sitting down on a wooden chair in her cabin, "we can talk openly now."

"Without the killer hearing us," Hawk added, watching the cabin door.

"Hawk," Nikki explained, "you may not believe me, but it was beneficial for us that the killer somehow listened in on our conversations. I'm confident that the killer recorded our every word."

Hawk watched Nikki lean forward and rest her face in her hands. "Nikki, don't lose steam on me," he said.

She drew in a deep breath. "The killer isn't Mr. Fench's son, Hawk. I think we have it backwards."

"How so?"

"You heard Matt—Mr. Fench's son drives around in a

Porsche. He's a country club brat. Why would he risk losing this diamond in the rough? This ship brings in good money. Look at the interior architecture. I don't believe this much money and effort was put into this ship simply to send it to the bottom of the sea. Also, did you notice that Dr. Rowen knew about Mr. Lane's past?"

Hawk rubbed his chin. "Nikki, are you saying Mr. Lane is the killer? That doesn't make any sense. That man needs money to take care of his wife. What would he gain from sinking this ship?"

"Exactly," Nikki told Hawk. Leaning up, she looked at Hawk with tired eyes. Fighting back a yawn, she glanced at the comfortable bed in her cabin. "Hawk, why did Captain Mayfield really hire Mr. Lane? If the man was crooked, he wouldn't just hire anyone. Mr. Lane was hired on as second-in-command for a reason."

Hawk took a minute to soak in the information Nikki was throwing at him. "But why would he want to sink this ship, Nikki? He has a sick wife."

"Right," Nikki said. "Hawk, I think Mr. Lane lied about his wife being home. I think that woman is right here on this ship. I think Mr. Lane is going to do something very horrible. You see his face, Hawk. He is tired, hurt, broken, and beaten down. I don't doubt he tried to go straight and live an honest life, but for the sake of his wife, he allowed Captain Mayfield to pull him back into a life of crime. I think he wants to end it all for himself and his wife, who may be much sicker than he's letting on."

"That theory is out there, Nikki."

"Hawk, after Dr. Rowen was murdered and you chased

after the killer, you didn't find him, did you? No. And when Mr. Lane saw Dr. Rowen's dead body, he had sweat on the side of his temples, like he had been running. Whoever the killer is, he knows this ship better than anyone. He understands how to maneuver without being seen or caught. Also, we both need to realize something that is vital, Hawk."

"What?"

"If the killer wanted us dead, we would be dead by now. Why would the killer give you a warning? He could easily have killed us at any moment, Hawk. The killer has only killed two men who knew him on a personal level."

Hawk looked at Nikki's beautiful face. He imagined Nikki being ill, suffering, hurting. And then he imagined his own life caught in a web of crime, forced to sit at the tables with common criminals against his will. When a man is desperate, he does desperate things. "I'm a cop—that must not sit well with him."

"That's why he wrote that fake note saying the killer told him to keep this ship on course. The handwriting on each piece of paper belongs to Mr. Lane, Hawk." Nikki pulled out the letter from the killer and the piece of paper she found on Dr. Rowen's body. "See the X I made with the pen I borrowed from Mr. Lane? I marked those papers with X's for a reason. Hawk, the ink from the pen Mr. Lane gave me matches the ink on the killer's letter, the paper I found on Dr. Rowen and the warning letter in the medical bay. When I used the bathroom a few minutes ago, I examined the papers."

"Could be anyone's pen. That won't hold up in a court

of law," Hawk warned Nikki as he examined the ink marks. "We need proof Lane is the killer."

"I wasn't sure Mr. Lane was the killer until a few minutes ago when we spoke with him on the bridge. "Mr. Lane didn't become upset when I mentioned the bomb to him. Hawk, he already knew that we were aware of the bomb. If you hadn't found the note in Dr. Rowen's brandy bottle..."

Hawk thought back to the warning letter. Nikki was right. If the killer wanted them dead, they would be dead. The two men who were dead knew Brody on a personal level. And, Hawk thought, Brody would know the layout of the ship as well as anyone. Closing his eyes, he saw the pain on Brody's face when the man confessed how poor his wife's health was. Was it possible Brody wanted to end it all for himself and his wife while at the same time sinking a ship and killing off anyone who might be able to incriminate him in a court of law? Anything was possible, Hawk concluded. "All right, Nikki, what's your game plan?"

"I've given it enough time," Nikki said, forcing her body to stand up. "Now we go to Mr. Lane's quarters."

"Shouldn't we find Matt, Tara, and Johnson? If Lane is the killer, he surely knows that we have those three searching for the bomb."

"They won't find the bomb," Nikki sighed. "If there was any chance they could, I'm afraid we wouldn't have found Mr. Lane on the bridge."

"Because he would have been out on a hunt." Hawk

quickly understood what Nikki was driving at. "Nikki, are you sure this man is the killer? I mean, are you certain?"

"Now I am," Nikki said in a miserable voice. "Hawk, I read his face. And his concern about this storm, it's all rehearsed, Hawk."

"But the conversation I heard him have with Mayfield during dinner, Nikki? Lane wasn't too keen on taking this ship through the storm."

"Hawk," Nikki said, "I've considered that conversation between Captain Mayfield and Mr. Lane. I think Mr. Lane manipulated Captain Mayfield. I'm certain there is some criminal cargo on this ship as we speak, that Captain Mayfield wanted to arrive at our vacation port. But you did say he told Mr. Lane to call around to other ports with the hopes that he could dock the ship until the storm passed."

"Yes, but Lane said the ports were all full."

"Were they?" Nikki asked. "Didn't you say that Captain Mayfield told Mr. Lane if no ports were available then they would ride the storm?"

"Yeah, he did say that," Hawk agreed. Like a man watching a strange puzzle come together, Hawk began to follow Nikki. "Lane manipulated Captain Mayfield. Lane wanted to make sure this ship was caught by the storm. So why kill Mayfield? The guy seemed to be on the same page with Lane's desire to take this ship into the storm."

"You," Nikki pointed at Hawk. "You make Mr. Lane nervous. I believe Mr. Lane was going to send everyone who knew him on a personal basis to the bottom of the ocean. But then you showed up, Hawk. Remember what

Captain Mayfield told us in the passenger lounge when he greeted us?"

Hawk thought back. "He said he was told that a man of the law would be taking this cruise," Hawk remembered.

"Kinda strange, don't you think, that he would say that? I mean, Hawk, I'm sorry, you're not exactly a world-famous detective."

"Hey, that's right." Hawk replied and then kicked himself. "Man, I'm getting slow in my old age. Nikki, are you sure you want a senile old man at your side?"

Nikki smiled. "I'm sure. Now," she said, getting serious, "I believe Mr. Lane killed Captain Mayfield to make you look away from him. Sleight-of-hand trick."

"Could have been," Hawk agreed. "And in order to keep us at sea, Lane writes that phony note, right?"

"Could be," Nikki agreed and then became very sad. "Hawk, Mr. Lane is a torn man. It's obvious he loves his wife. It's also obvious he's a man beaten down, ripped apart in his heart, defeated. Maybe his life was going well when he was captain of the *Blue Pearl,* and maybe he was the scapegoat as he claims. I think it's possible—otherwise, why would he crawl under Captain Mayfield's thumb?"

"That's no excuse for murder, Nikki."

"I agree, but when a man has nothing else to lose because he's already losing everything..." Nikki stopped talking. Tears began to fall from her eyes. Walking over to Hawk, she threw her arms around him and began crying. "I've lost it all once too, Hawk," she cried. "I loved my ex-husband, I truly did. He ripped my heart out."

"It's okay, let it out," Hawk soothed Nikki, gently

embracing her. Nikki cried until it hurt. "Cry all you want, you hear me?"

When Nikki was able to control her tears, she leaned up and looked Hawk in the eyes. Wiping at her tears, she sighed. "Hawk, love makes a person's actions become very unstable and desperate when that person believes he or she is losing everything. I know Mr. Lane's murderous actions are not justified...it's just that I feel so sorry for him. I understand how he feels. When a marriage ends, it's like one spouse is dying of a terminal disease."

"I know," Hawk agreed. "I was married once, too. But Nikki, right now, we have innocent lives to save."

Nikki wiped at her tears some more. "I guess we better get to Mr. Lane's quarters. He should be there with his wife. We have to be careful, though."

"He might detonate the bomb," Hawk warned.

"I don't think so. Not now, anyway. I think Mr. Lane is waiting for something."

Hawk stared at Nikki. "Yeah?" he asked. "Nikki, you seem awful calm for a woman who knows full well there is a bomb that could go off on this ship at any minute."

Nikki scratched her nose. "Hawk, when I shook Mr. Lane's hand, I did so for a reason. I wanted to see the man's watch. His watch is stopped exactly at midnight, two hours from now. I think that's when the bomb will detonate."

Hawk whistled in the air. "You are a sly one," he told Nikki, "but still, Nikki, it could be that the man's watch just stopped."

Nikki gave Hawk a 'do-you-really-believe-that?' look. "We better get to Mr. Lane's cabin. I'm sure he'll be there by now. I've spooked him, Hawk. From here on out, I doubt he'll be on the bridge. He's going to avoid me at all costs."

"Okay," Hawk said, taking out his gun. "Let's go trap a rat."

"Not a rat," Nikki corrected Hawk. "Mr. Lane is a man who is simply very disturbed."

"Disturbed or not, he's a killer, Nikki. Let's go."

15

"My dear," Brody said, placing a cold washcloth onto the forehead of a delicate Chinese woman lying very ill on a soft, king-sized bed, "it won't be long now before your suffering will end. I've gone through great trouble to get where we are right now, but it was worth it. We're together—we'll be together forever."

The Chinese woman, resting unconsciously in a pink robe, didn't reply. Instead, she moaned painfully in her sleep. Brody brushed a sweaty bang from her eyes. "That woman, that Ms. Bates, she's a clever one. She has me all figured out. I saw that when I was up on the bridge," he told his wife in an angry, bitter voice. "But they won't find the bomb. And they won't escape this storm. Oh yes, I've put us right in the middle of this storm, honey. No one will escape; everyone will perish along with us. It has to be that way. Too many crew members understand who I am. They think I'm a putz; they think I'm responsible for sinking the

Blue Pearl. Oh, they'll pay, with their lives. I've got the bomb set just right. When it explodes, the sea will rush in and pull us under, I promise. Two hours to go..."

Brody stood up, walked into the bathroom connected to his small cabin, doused the washcloth with cold water again, and returned to his wife. "We're almost to the spot where we first met, remember?" he asked his wife, sitting down on the edge of the bed. Taking a deep breath of the menthol vapor rub he had massaged onto his wife's chest, Brody smiled down at his wife's sleeping face as tears began to fall from his eyes. "I went out on deck to get some fresh air. It was midnight. The moon was full. I saw you standing alone. Oh, you were so beautiful, honey...I fell in love with you right then and there."

Brody wiped at his tears. "Not long now, honey. We're going to die in the same spot we met. Well, maybe not the same spot, but close. This storm is throwing us off course a little, but no matter." Brody sighed. "You know, I really didn't want to kill Mayfield or Rowen, but that cop—Daily... He didn't know, but I saw him listening when I spoke with Mayfield outside the dining room about the storm. I had to play it real cool, honey, real cool." Brody paused and then sighed miserably. "Oh, who am I kidding? I panicked. I killed Mayfield because I was scared that cop was sent on board to arrest me—foolish paranoia. But if I killed Mayfield, then attention would be taken off me, don't you see? And then Rowen, he caught me checking on the bomb in the medical bay. I had to kill him, honey, you see? I had to. I've been real smart. I've managed to keep us on course, give or take, and so what if that nosy woman knows about the bomb. What can they do about it? Sure, they sent that brat kid looking for my bomb, but he'll never find it."

Confused and angry, Brody stood up and began to pace around his cabin. The cabin was small, cramped and filled with cheap furnishings. "Ugly room," Brody fussed, running his hands through his hair. Shaking his head, he stopped pacing and looked at his wife. "I never could lie to you, could I? You're seeing straight through me. You always could. The truth is, honey, I'm cracking up. Sure, I knew that cop overheard my talk with Mayfield, but so what? What could he really do? I killed Mayfield because I wanted to, because I despised the man. I panicked afterward, and that's when I wrote that note. I knew that cop would insist I take this ship back to port. And Rowen, I could have handled him differently, but..." Brody balled his hands into two tight fists. "He mocked me, he always mocked me. He deserved to die. They all do, don't you see? They all mock me, honey. They think I'm a joke—sure, good ol' Brody, the man who sank the *Blue Pearl* and became the lackey of a criminal."

Brody punched the left wall of his cabin. Then he looked at his wife. Feeling his anger intensify, he punched the wall again. "Mayfield knew I needed money for your treatments, but did he care? No. As long as I did as he told me and made sure his precious cargo was delivered into the hands of thieves and criminals, I got paid. He didn't care that you were dying—no one does! No one cares that your doctor has given you a year to live, to live in pain and misery. No, I had to end it, honey. Tonight, we die together, and those people who mocked me, they will suffer their fate."

Brody walked back to his wife's bed and sat down. As he did, Hawk kicked open the cabin door. "Freeze!" he yelled at Brody.

Taken off guard, Brody jumped to his feet. Startled, he stared at Hawk. His mind quickly jumped into action. "What is this all about? How dare you?" he yelled. "My wife is a very sick woman!"

Nikki eased past Hawk. "Mr. Lane," she pleaded, "we know you set the bomb. We know you killed Captain Mayfield and Dr. Rowen. Please, don't take any more innocent lives."

Feeling a click in his mind, Brody exploded. "Innocent lives? What about my wife's life?!" he yelled at Nikki. "Look at her! She's suffering! And who cares? Did Mayfield or Rowen care? Yes, I killed them, and I enjoyed it. And tonight, everyone will suffer, the same way my wife has suffered!"

"Where is the bomb, Lane?" Hawk demanded.

"At midnight you'll find out," Brody yelled at Hawk. Sitting down on the bed, he took his wife's hand. "Place me under arrest, but allow me to stay at my wife's side. I'm not going anywhere. I want to die at her side, holding her hand. We will drown together as husband and wife."

Nikki drew in a deep breath. Walking over to a flimsy wooden chest, she carefully lifted the lid. Bending down, she reached in and retrieved three bamboo darts and a small glass medical vial holding a deadly green poison. "Mr. Lane," she said, standing up, "Let me help you. It's obvious you have had a nervous breakdown. Detective Daily and I will help you if—"

"Help me?" Brody interrupted Nikki, lowering his voice almost to a whisper. "Lady, you're the one that needs help. Your only chance is to get up to the lifeboats. But even if you did get off the ship, the sea would swallow you up. You see, I've made sure no one can escape. I want everyone to suffer the same way my wife and I have been suffering. Oh, they'll pay. They'll all pay."

Hawk lowered his gun. It was clear to him that Brody was no longer a physical threat. As Nikki had claimed, the man was broken, mentally and emotionally. Desperate to save innocent lives, Hawk spotted a Bible lying on a wooden desk. Calmly, he walked over to the desk and picked it up with his left hand. "Your wife is a Christian?" he asked.

"Yes," Brody answered raising his eyes to Hawk. "Put down my wife's Bible, do you hear me?"

"Is this what she would want from you?" Hawk asked Brody. "Before you answer me, look down into your wife's face and ask yourself, is this what she wants?"

Brody lowered his eyes onto his wife's lovely face. Suddenly, tears began falling from his eyes. "She's dying, and no one cared. I want them all to suffer the way she has suffered, the way I have suffered. They've mocked me, and I've had to withstand the pain because I needed money to pay for my wife's medical treatments. I've become a criminal, Detective, and you dare ask me is this what my wife wants? At least now it's all coming to an end. I'm doing this for her."

"Killing innocent people isn't what your wife wants,"

Nikki told Brody in a caring voice. "Mr. Lane, please, let us help you."

Brody shook his head no. "At midnight this ship and everyone aboard is going to die. And who will hear their cries? Who will hear their screams? No one—just like no one heard my cries and my screams."

Hawk walked over to Brody and handed him his wife's Bible. "Take the Bible," he said.

Brody took his wife's Bible. "Leave us alone," he told Hawk.

"Come on, Nikki," Hawk said, "let's leave them alone. There's nothing we can do here. Our best bet is to search for the bomb."

Nikki placed the bamboo darts and poison into the front pocket of her dress. "I'm sorry, Mr. Lane, for your suffering. You may not believe that, but I am."

Nikki began to walk away, but a weak, faint voice began speaking. "No...don't." Brody's wife spoke in a pained voice. "Brody..."

"It's okay, I'm here," Brody promised his wife, taking her hand. "You rest, honey. Everything is okay."

"No...bomb...heaven...we won't...together…" Brody's wife said as her eyes struggled to open. Unable to open her eyes, the woman began breathing heavily. "Heaven...promise...don't...bomb..." And then the woman stopped breathing altogether.

"No!" Brody yelled, jumping to his feet. Putting the Bible down on the bed, he began doing CPR on his wife. "Help me—somebody help me!" he yelled as tears stormed from his eyes.

Hawk grabbed Brody, pushed him aside, and yelled at Nikki, "You breathe for her; I'll do the chest compressions."

Nikki jumped into action. Running to the bed, she carefully got into place as Hawk began doing chest compressions on the dead woman. "No..." Brody cried, backing up to the left wall. "No!" Feeling his spirit begin to die, he watched as Hawk and Nikki worked to bring his wife back to life. And then, just when all hope was lost, Nikki yelled, "She's breathing!"

"What?" Brody yelled and ran back to his wife. Looking down at the bed, he saw his wife begin breathing on her own. "But how? She..."

Hawk placed a caring hand on Brody's shoulder. "People do care," he said, breathing hard. "We may all die tonight, Lane, but not everyone who is going to die is your enemy."

Brody slowly turned his head and looked at Hawk. He didn't see a man who was his enemy. Instead, he saw a decent, honest man—the type of man he himself used to be. Looking down at his wife, at her pale, sick face, he began to cry. "My wife has one year to live."

"Let us help you," Hawk pleaded with Brody. "Let us be your friends."

"You'll send me to prison," Brody said. Through his tears, he glanced down at the gun Hawk had shoved down into the belt holster on his hip before doing CPR on his wife. With fast hands, he grabbed the gun. "Get out," he told Hawk and Nikki, aiming the gun at Hawk's chest. "I don't want to hurt you, but if you don't get out, I will kill you both."

Hawk stared into Brody's eyes. It was clear the man was insane, suffering from a dysfunctional emotional state that had transformed him into a deadly killer. "Come on Nikki, let's—"

"Wait!" Brody yelled, turning the gun in his hands to Nikki. "Give me back my poison. I don't want to hurt you, but I'm sorry, you both have to die. I can't let you walk out of here alive."

Nikki looked at Hawk. Hawk bit down on his lower lip. Kicking himself for allowing his gun to be taken, he desperately searched for a way out but could find no exit. Watching Brody ease over to the cabin door to close it, he knew once the door was closed, he and Nikki were both dead. That's when a hand reached through the door, smacked the gun out of Brody's hand and then punched the man in the face. Brody stumbled backward toward Hawk. Hawk grabbed him and slung him down onto the floor. "Good timing," he told Herbert, placing handcuffs on Brody.

Herbert stepped into the cabin with Lidia following behind him. "My wife and I have talked," he told Nikki in an apologetic voice. "Can you forgive me for being a fool?"

Nikki ran to Herbert and hugged him. "You're my hero, not a fool," she said.

"How did you two know we were here?" Hawk asked.

"We went to the bridge," Lidia explained. "A nice man said that Mr. Lane had gone to check on the passengers, but most likely would check on his wife first. He told us what deck Mr. Lane's cabin was on."

Nikki let go of Herbert and hugged Lidia. "We still have a bomb to worry about."

"You'll never find the bomb," Brody yelled. "Everyone is going to die; everyone is going to suffer."

"Medical…" Brody's wife struggled to speak.

Nikki ran to the bed. "Ma'am, can you hear me? Please, where is the bomb?"

"Medical..." Brody's wife managed to say through heavy breaths, "Rowen..." Unable to say any more, the woman fell unconscious.

"Medical? Rowen?" Nikki whispered, checking the woman's pulse with loving hands. "Her pulse is weak but stable."

"What was she trying to tell us?" Hawk asked Nikki.

Herbert and Lidia looked at each other for answers but were unable to help. "All I heard her say was the word 'medical' and the name 'Rowen,'" Lidia told Hawk.

Nikki stared down at Brody's wife, into the woman's sleeping face. "Medical...Rowen..." she whispered, and then the answer came to her. "The bomb is in the medical bay! Hawk, go find Mr. Johnson and meet me there. Lidia, Herbert, stay here and watch Mr. Lane and his wife."

Before Herbert or Lidia could respond, Nikki was already on her feet and dashing out of the cabin. On nervous legs, she rushed through the ship, fighting to stay balanced as the ship struggled through the stormy sea like a battered soldier trying to make his way back to a safe foxhole. When she reached the medical bay, she rushed in. Ignoring Captain Mayfield's and Dr. Rowen's bodies, she stood very still as her eyes searched the medical bay. "Where could the bomb be?" she asked herself.

Cautiously, she walked around without touching anything as her eyes wandered. "Where would you hide a bomb, Mr. Lane?" Nikki asked aloud. Feeling cold air coming down from the metal duct attached to the ceiling, Nikki looked up. Spotting three vents attached to the metal duct, she raised her hands into the air. Something wasn't right. The vent she was standing under, the vent closest to the door, was pushing out a steady stream of air. But when she walked past the vent located at the back of the medical bay, Nikki felt no cold air.

Curiously, she walked back to the vent located on the back wall and raised her hands. No air was coming from the vent. "Something is blocking the air from coming out..." Feeling fear grip her stomach, Nikki ran to the desk, grabbed the desk chair, and dragged it back to the vent. Praying for good balance, she stood up on the chair, reached up, and, with scared hands, removed the metal vent covering without much struggle. Dropping the vent covering down onto the floor, Nikki placed her hands against the metal duct for better balance, leaned up onto her tippy-toes, and peered into it. And there, sitting in the duct, was a bomb, glowing with red and green lights.

"Nikki!" Hawk yelled, running into the medical bay with Mr. Johnson behind him.

"It's here—the bomb is here," she told Hawk, easing down from the chair. With shaky arms, she hugged Hawk. "I'm terrified."

Embracing Nikki, Hawk nodded at Lei Johnson. "Do what you can."

Matt and Tara appeared at the doorway. "Clever," Matt said in an angry voice. "I would have never looked in here."

Lei, now carrying a black briefcase holding his diamonds, looked up at the metal duct. Drawing in a steady breath, he put the briefcase down onto the floor, walked over to the chair Nikki had dragged over, and stood up on it. Peering into the duct, he spotted the bomb. "Everyone out," he ordered.

"Come on," Hawk said, walking Nikki out of the medical bay and closing the door. "All we can do now is pray."

Nikki pulled Tara to her side and hugged her. "Matt, take Tara and get topside. If anything, you two can try and make it to a lifeboat if that bomb goes off."

Tara hugged Nikki. "Thank you for being so kind," she said.

"Let's move," Matt said, grabbing Tara.

Hawk took Nikki's hand. "I would tell you to leave, but I know you won't."

"And you won't leave that man inside the medical bay to die alone," Nikki told Hawk, staring into his eyes. "If we ever make it back home, I want to have dinner with you at the diner. I want to cuddle in front of the fireplace with you and eat chocolates that we make together."

Hawk smiled, leaned forward, and gently kissed Nikki. "If we ever get home," he smiled, "it may be wise not to let Pop know about any of this."

Nikki tried to smile but failed. Instead, she leaned her head against Hawk's chest and waited. Silence fell on the hallway. Outside, the stormy seas continued to batter the ship. Nikki checked her watch. Hawk did the same. "Give him time," he told Nikki, expecting to be blown to pieces at any second.

Nikki pressed her head harder against Hawk's chest and wrapped her arms around him. Closing her eyes, she brought her son's face into her mind. If anything happened to her... Feeling tears begin to fall, Nikki began to pray as the minutes ticked away.

At ten minutes before midnight, just when Hawk believed all hope was lost, Lei Johnson opened the door to the medical bay. Carrying his briefcase, he tipped a wink at Hawk, then walked away. "Wait," Hawk ordered, "what about the bomb?"

"Sitting on the desk, harmless," Lei called back over his shoulder. "Oh, by the way, anytime you want to go one-on-one, you just let me know."

"Should we?" Hawk asked Nikki.

Nikki nodded and took Hawk's hand, then they both eased into the medical bay. And there, sitting on the desk, was the bomb, disabled and dead. "How did he do it?" Nikki asked.

"Who knows and who cares? Just be grateful that we had the right tool in the toolbox," Hawk said, wiping sweat from his head and then laughing. "Oh boy, Nikki, I thought we were goners for sure."

Nikki, feeling a tidal wave of relief wash over her, began laughing, too. Suddenly, the dangerous storm outside the ship seemed like a gentle summer rain, even though the ship did feel like it was about to be dragged down under the ocean at any second. But Nikki doubted the ship was going to give up its fight to stay alive. Sometimes an old clunker outperformed the best of the best. "Hawk, someday when you propose to me, propose to me on dry ground."

"You can count on that," Hawk laughed. Hugging Nikki, he closed his eyes. Boy, did he ever need a vacation.

16

"Oh, it's so good to be home," Nikki said, dancing around her store. She took in the scent of delicious chocolates that floated in the air. "I'm never leaving home again."

"Me neither," Lidia agreed, locking the door to the store behind her. Dressed in a white shirt and a tan skirt, she felt ready to dive into a good day of work and forget all about the cruise.

Nikki walked around the store, running her fingers over the wooden shelves and chocolates. She felt alive and happy. Her son was coming home for a visit. Tori was attending her first college class. Herbert liked her. Lidia was at her side. Hawk was going to take her to the diner for lunch. Life was good.

Smoothing the front of the green dress she was wearing, Nikki looked down at herself. Here stood a woman that had faced danger toe-to-toe on many occasions, yet there she stood, alive and vibrant. "Lidia?" she asked.

"Yeah?" Lidia asked, unlocking the office door.

"I've decided not to take the job at the paper."

Lidia froze. "Oh?" she asked, looking back at Nikki.

Nikki smiled. Walking behind the front counter, she took out a piece of peppermint chocolate and began to nibble on it. "Actually, I'm going to write a book. I know a publisher in Atlanta who I can contact. Her name is Noel Bakersfield. Noel was always after me to write a mystery book."

"You've never told me that, honey," Lidia said, giving Nikki a curious eye. "I wonder what else you haven't told me?"

Nikki laughed. "You know all of my secrets, I promise."

Lidia smiled, took the piece of peppermint chocolate from Nikki, and began to eat it. "So, no job at the paper?"

"No," Nikki explained. "Lidia," she said, examining her chocolate store with loving eyes, "I feel that...well, I feel that someday Hawk is going to ask me to marry him."

"That's obvious," Lidia replied, polishing off the peppermint chocolate.

Nikki blushed a little. "Well," she said, "after all we've been through, I don't really have the desire to chase after crime anymore. I see myself sitting at home on a cold, snowy day, drinking hot chocolate and writing a book. I can't see myself scurrying all over town trying to dig up one story after another. I'm not getting any younger."

Lidia watched Nikki speak. Her gut told her Nikki wasn't telling her something. "Honey, what is it? You can confide in me."

Continuing to examine the store, Nikki opened up even more. "We all could have died on that ship, Lidia. When

Hawk and I were standing in the hallway outside the medical bay, waiting to live or die, I thought of my son. What would have happened if Mr. Johnson hadn't been able to disable the bomb? What would have happened if you and Herbert hadn't shown up when you did? Mr. Lane would surely have killed me and Hawk."

"That man is behind bars now," Lidia promised Nikki, "and his poor wife is in a hospital where she belongs."

"I know," Nikki said. "Lidia, my son means the world to me. I moved to Vermont to escape a life that always placed us in danger. And look at me, I arrive in town like a hot-headed reporter who can't keep her nose out of trouble."

Lidia approached Nikki, gently patted her shoulder, and smiled. "You are who you are, honey. Don't deny your talent. If you want to write books, wonderful. But don't pass up a job at the paper, either. This town needs you, Nikki. This town needs a woman who will search for the truth no matter what. You have a gifted mind and don't ever forget that."

"But what about my son?" Nikki asked.

"Well," Lidia said in a loving, motherly tone, "our children will live their lives and we, their parents, must live our lives. And don't forget, you have me at your side. I'll keep you out of trouble."

Hearing someone knock at the front door, Nikki knew it was Hawk by the cute knocking pattern he liked to do. Hugging Lidia, she walked to the front door and unlocked it. Hawk appeared, wearing a bright orange hockey jersey. "Donuts?" he asked, carrying a white paper bag.

"Oh, Hawk," Nikki shielded her eyes against the bright orange jersey, "you're going to send me into shock."

"Very funny," Hawk said, stepping into the store. "Oh, by the way, Lane's wife was transferred to a hospital in Los Angeles. I spoke with a doctor there. He said it might be touch and go for a while, but it's possible she might live out a full life. The hospital is going to try a new experimental drug."

"That's wonderful," Nikki said, reaching into the bag and taking out a glazed donut. "What about Mr. Lane, Hawk? What will happen to him?"

"Well," Hawk said, taking a bite of a powdered donut and getting some on his face, "Lane's lawyer has marked him as a fruitcake. The courts bought it, hook, line, and sinker. Lane is going to be transferred from the jail he's being held at to a mental hospital for the criminally insane in Seattle."

"Good," Nikki said, walking back to the front counter.

"Need I remind you that nutcase was going to kill us?" Hawk told Nikki, following behind her.

"I know," Nikki said as she began to inventory the chocolates with her eyes, "but Hawk, I can't help but feel sorry for Mr. Lane. I know, I know, he killed two people, and for that, he deserves to spend the rest of his life in a mental hospital where he can't hurt anyone else. But you saw how much he loved his wife."

Hawk decided not to place his case out on the line. What was done was done. The important thing was that innocent lives were saved, the bad guy was where he belonged, and he was back home with Nikki. "Let's forget about Lane," Hawk told Nikki and finished off his donut. "The real reason I came by is because I have some bad news."

"Bad news?" Nikki asked.

"I have to drive down to New York tomorrow. An old friend of mine was shot. I want to see him. I was wondering," Hawk paused and scratched the back of his head, "if you might like to come?"

Lidia stuck her head out of the office. "Yes, she would mind. Nikki is staying put where I can keep an eye on her."

"Lidia is right, Hawk. I really do need to focus on the store, and I still haven't reported to the paper, yet. I would love to come, but I want to stay home. Please don't be upset."

"Oh, no, I'm not upset," Hawk promised Nikki. "Well," he said and quickly kissed Nikki goodbye, "I better get some work done today before Pop cans me. I'll see you for lunch."

"Okay." Nikki smiled and let Hawk out. Leaning against the front door, she closed her eyes. "You big lug, how are you going to go to New York alone?"

"Oh no," Lidia said, rushing up to Nikki. "I want you where I can see you."

"He's so helpless, though," Nikki told Lidia. "Maybe I better go with him. Someone has to take care of the big lug. I mean, you see the way he dresses. The man obviously needs help."

"We all need help," Lidia sighed and then laughed. "All right, go to New York with Hawk. Just stay out of trouble."

Nikki laughed. "We'll try. But honestly, Lidia, maybe a crime-infested city is the safest place to be."

Lidia thought about Nikki's statement. She diffidently agreed.

Outside, the morning continued to blossom under a soft, warm, blue sky as the world woke up.

ABOUT THE AUTHOR

Wendy Meadows is the USA Today bestselling author of many novels and novellas, from cozy mysteries to clean, sweet romances. Check out her popular cozy mystery series Sweetfern Harbor, Alaska Cozy and Sweet Peach Bakery, just to name a few.

If you enjoyed this book, please take a few minutes to leave a review. Authors truly appreciate this, and it helps other readers decide if the book might be for them. Thank you!

Get in touch with Wendy

www.wendymeadows.com

amazon.com/author/wendymeadows

goodreads.com/wendymeadows

bookbub.com/authors/wendy-meadows

facebook.com/AuthorWendyMeadows

twitter.com/wmeadowscozy

This is a work of fiction. Names, characters, places, and incidents are a product of the author's imagination. Locales and public names are sometimes used for atmospheric purposes. Any resemblance to actual people, living or dead, or to businesses, companies, events, institutions, or locales is completely coincidental.

Printed in the United States of America

www.ingramcontent.com/pod-product-compliance
Lightning Source LLC
La Vergne TN
LVHW012110160826
845678LV00014B/3021

* 9 7 8 1 5 4 4 1 4 4 0 9 2 *